ABRAHAM ANYHOW

A Novel

By Adam Van Winkle

Cover and Interior Design: Greg Gilpin, Graphic Art Center, Inc.

Red Dirt Press
1831 N. Park Ave.
Shawnee, OK 74804
www.reddirtpress.net
www.adamvanwinkle.com

ISBN-978-0-692-85341-2

CONTENTS

For Orin Van Winkle, and all that we share.
Thanks for the stories. Love you, Dad.

For Constance Beitzel, my love, for the language
we've made all our own. My heart is yours.

Abraham took the wood of the burnt offering and put it upon Isaac his son and took in his hands the fire and the slaughtering knife, and both of them went on together.
--Genesis 22:6

THE BULLDOG AND THE SNAKE

FRIDAY

The day was hot with noontime sun. Abe's Bronco brought a cloud of dust with it into the diner's gravel lot. The dust blew past Abe as he stepped from the driver's side door.

He had spotted one of the Sledge boys' trucks in the lot of the diner from a quarter mile or a little less but hadn't bothered to brake until he was practically through the big plate glass window of the diner's dining room.

Just as Abraham Dyson crawled out of the cab and shut the heavy door, Shane and Alistair Sledge came out of the diner's double doors and into the steamy limestone lot. Abe stopped and leaned on the hood of the Sledges' old orange GMC pickup and pulled a cigarette to light.

"You sure got big breeches leaning on my truck while you're still holdin' the other ransom."

"Impound ain't the same as ransom and you damn well know it Sledge." Despite the hot approach into the parking lot, Abe was playing it very cool. He'd impounded the truck two nights past when OHP picked up Randy Sledge for speeding and driving with whiskey breath. Abe exhaled Marlboro Red. The Bronco ticked and clicked as the oil pan and engine pulleys and muffler and all cooled after the fast drive into town.

"Watcha doin' sittin' on my truck now?"

"This one yours yours, or just in the family? I don't keep up with which one of you is driving what these days—especially since y'all always seem to travel in a pack most of the time," Abe said, smiling and nodding at Allie who had yet to speak through his dumb and slightly agape mouth.

"Comes down to it, they're all mine," Shane said, lighting his own cigarette.

"Well go figure," Abe said before getting to the point. "I come to town cuz I need to see a Sledge and looks like I have the ringleader right here."

"The fuck you want, Abe?" Shane shot back, also trying to get to the point.

"Besides the impound fee for that piece of shit so I can clean it out of my lot, wondering if you know anything about King not being back at the shop this mornin'?"

"I ain't got him if that's what you mean." Shane seemed genuinely surprised.

"Didn't think you did Shane. But since ol' Hoyt saw that ragged ass Scout that Andy and Randy usually run around in trolling around my lot last night, it got me thinkin' since Randy's the one got arrested and got that old truck impounded and there's forty or fifty pounds of dog food in an open box covering God knows what inside that tinted camper on the back, maybe these two dipshits were snoopin' around to steal the truck and when they couldn't figure my fence and lock, they loaded up my dog instead. Like some dumbass kidnappin' and ransom plot to trade?"

Shane was looking down at the gravel getting redder as Abe painted the picture.

"Like I said," Abe continued, "just wondering if you knew anything about anything like that."

"I, surely, do, not," Shane Sledge replied, listing his words to underscore his point.

Abe aped in reply: "No, maybe, you, don't, know, shit." Then he tacked on, "Don't seem to most times I run into you. Not your brothers or cousins neither. Must be a family condition—not knowing shit." Again Abe nodded in Allie's direction and Allie dully stared back, breathing through his mouth.

Shane continued for both of them: "Alright Dyson—find Andy or Randy then. Leave us alone."

"I could spend my day doing that, but how about this? You tell those assholes to bring King and the money for that mule in my pin. If they don't, I'll call one of my uniformed buddies and have 'em sift through that Purina in the back."

"Why you think I give such a shit about Randy's problem anyway?"

"I took the liberty of checkin' the glovebox—wrecker's privilege. It's registered to your mom—she's going to have to sift through a pile of shit for that alone if it comes up a drug runner."

"Damn you, Dyson."

"Be pissy with your brothers. I'd just assumed filed for salvage on the truck after 90 days. But those morons had to get ideas of their own."

"What if they don't have King—or if—"

"Just get him back."

Shane was beat by the box in the back of the truck but still wanted to lash out. He shoved his brother. "Go back in there and call Randy and Andy. Tell them to get the damn dog back out to Dyson's place."

Alistair thought he was still supposed to play dumb because he really was dumb: "What if they don't have the dog, Shane?"

"Just fucking go," Shane snapped. After a beat he tried to make peace to a degree: "I told Randy he had to take care of it since he got into that shit. Abe, I meant for him to pay you, honest. He got other ideas apparently."

"Apparently—least I ain't ever known Hoyt to tell stories."

"Nah—get that old you got no reason to lie to yourself or others about what you see."

Abe studied Shane's acne scarred face, burned red by the Oklahoma sun, and his juvenile haircut as out of step with his age as the bright white basketball sneakers he wore. As he studied Shane, Abe realized this Sledge always did have the most sense, even if he looked like all the rest. They finished their cigarettes. Abe lit another.

As Allie came back out of the diner, Abe offered clear terms. "Alright," he said, shifting his stance and holding his lighter like a tommyhawk at Shane, "we just wanna say Randy made a kindhearted mistake—picked up a stray with the best of intentions—didn't know where he belonged. Long as King makes his way back, all it ever needs to look like."

Allie, still the bluntest Sledge, thought he had an insight and had to share: "Everyone knows that's your pup, Abraham Dyson."

"Well, I'm sure you'll figure out something, Alistair,

to help your brothers find their way to get my dog back to-day."

Shane cut off whatever reply was slowly working its way out of Allie's slack jaw: "No problem, Abe."

"Bring money for that mule too—it's takin' up space in the yard." Abe pocketed his lighter.

"Yea," Shane shot back. Abe wasn't sure if it was real or a brush off but didn't want to stir the shit anymore for the moment.

The ride back was hot and dusty as the white gravel resin from the diner's lot blew off the hood of the Bronco and over the black hairs of Abe's big mechanic's arm as he rested it on the open window and made the turn onto the two-lane back to the shop. The Bronco's glasspacks rumbled as Abe accelerated.

Lee "Wild Child" Pitchman was waiting in the shop office, sitting on an old van bench seat tack-welded to a couple of rusty jackstands that worked as a couch. Lee had a tinfoil bag of greasy chicken strips in his hands and a big Styrofoam cup of tea was crotched between his legs. He was Abe's buddy since school.

"Y'anna chicken strip?" he asked offering the greasy bag at Abe.

"Yea, gimme one, I didn't grab anything to eat in town." Abe reached and poached one of the pieces of chicken. Afterwards he slid the moist soft pack out of his sweat-soaked shirt pocket and pulled a Marlboro from it before returning it and lighting the cigarette.

"Reach me that lighter," Lee said, breaking Abe out of a sort of spell once he'd smoked the cigarette about a third of the way. In the meantime, Lee had rolled a cigarette from his pack of cheap Bugler having set the bag of strips aside to

11

enjoy the early afternoon smoke with Abe. When he'd got his stringy cigarette lit and inhaled deeply, he asked with the exhale, trying not to be too eager, "Find King or the Sledges?"

"Run into Allie and Shane as it happened—made it clear I'd take the dog and impound fees on that truck by the end of the day." Abe didn't elaborate and Lee took the hint not to ask anymore.

For his part, Abe simply didn't want to spend anymore worry on it until he'd give Shane time to keep to his word.

After lunch King normally lounged in the shop's office. The dog'd report back to the property sometime early to mid morning after running all night. Sometime around 9 every night, after dinner, when Abe was watching TV, the dog would go to the door and stand until Abe let the big beast out. Some nights there'd be a dog or two waiting on the porch for King to be let out. Other nights, King ran up Duff Avenue and out of sight on his own. When Abe came out of the house in the morning with coffee and cigarette on his way to the shop at the north end of his lot, King was liable to be curled up on the porch. Otherwise, he'd be around within an hour or so of Abe starting work, lounging on the van seat couch in the office to recover from the night. At the end of the workday, the dog followed Abe back up to the house to be fed and nap near Abe's chair until night come and he wanted out again. A time or two, the dog had come back snake bit. A time or two, he'd come back shot for roaming on the wrong property no doubt. But he was tough and big to boot, and it never slowed him more than a day or two from his usual routine.

King come by his name by a holiday. Tradition around the Dyson property named dogs after the closest holiday to the pup's adoption. There'd been Candy Cane, a female German Shepherd mix picked up on the side of the road one December. There was Valentine, another pit bull from a litter of one of Abe's customer's one February. Dogs didn't have long life spans around the lot. Though treated supremely by their owner, there was just too much car movement, antifreeze, oil, and other dog killers around the shop for them to last long. Naming them after the nearest holiday gave a practical way of naming the dog without getting too personal.

When they did pass, their owner mourned their loss and buried them on the lot. Abe found it wasn't easy to dig a dog grave in a gravel lot, but he did them that much. Then he'd take the next free pup that come along that he thought'd make a good shop dog and needed a home. He was a believer that property with an impound oughtta have a tough looking dog. Even if the mutt would stay in the house too.

The pit bull King was brought by Wild Child after Valentine was run over for sleeping under the wrong Cummings diesel. Its emergency brake had give and even though the roll was slight the tire caught Valentine's neck just right. Or wrong. Lee found King abandoned on a country road out by his small property a week later in late January, around six months old and a little underweight though clearly destined to be a big pit. Naturally he thought he'd found Abe's next shop dog.

"Martin" didn't fit the young beast so "King" was the clear choice with MLK Day the closest holiday on the calendar.

Abe wouldn't have really been all that worked up about finding the damn dog around lunch this day and flown to town to find the Sledges—he'd of allowed the dog more grace period than that to return home. But Hoyt wasn't one to lie and Abe bet right on the old man's word that if confronted, the Sledge clan wouldn't deny it.

As he finished his cigarette, Abe grew almost nauseous. Dealings with the Sledges was never easy, and there'd be trouble this time too, of some sort, if odds had their way.

Abe returned to work, recharging air conditioners, replacing burst hoses, and replacing stuck thermostats—all common jobs this time year brought on by the summer heat and swelter. Lee piddled around on his own truck out in the gravel shop yard. The truck was a contraption of his own devising being half '54 Ford pickup and half '85 Chevy Blazer. Abe worked away in the shop stalls. The temperature was the same inside as out—107—owing to the baking effect of a corrugated tin building on top of a concrete slab in the Oklahoma sun.

Late afternoon found Abe again resting in the shop's office with a cigarette and coffee. He was contemplating the framed picture of his dad's old circle track Chevy that sat on his desk. Abe's father had built it and played in it on weekends when he wasn't turning wrenches for a living himself. He'd picked up the trade in World War II working on dozer and ship and plane engines. Abe learned from his dad.

"What's your old lady gonna think about this whole thing with the dog?" Lee's question again pulled Abe out of a sort of spell.

Abe hadn't thought about Sara in the hubbub of the day. She loved the dog—would be okay with Abe doing what he had to get it back. She'd worry but she generally trusted Abe.

"She'll just be glad we haven't lost King. IF I tell her."

Lee wasn't sure why Abe wouldn't tell her, but never having been successfully married himself, he didn't question it. Instead he offered, without any real reason to doubt and only in neat parallel to Abe's last thought, "IF you get him back."

"They won't try to pull nothin' with the dog. Least I don't think so."

On cue, King came leisurely strolling into the open shop bay on the north side of the building. Abe and Lee saw him through the window that looked from the office into the work stalls. They went from the office into the shop to see closer.

"What the hell? Where they at?" Lee asked as he bent to scratch the completely unexcited dog.

"Yonder," Abe said and pointed his cigarette to the end of his gravel lot through the shop's big bay door. The Sledges' Scout was pulling away on its bald tires. "Guess they didn't scrape together enough for the truck."

Lee looked at his longtime friend. Abe never got worked up. He might even be called unshakable, Abe Dyson. Lee thought about the night at the biker bar in Kingston, when they were young.

Kingston was bigger than Oakland by a good measure and smaller than Madill by about the same.

Abe and Lee got off over there one night sometime after they'd been out of high school a few years and before either was thinking of being married. They were going to a biker bar. Abe and Lee had gone to school with the owner's son and had been in there a few times when their former classmate worked barback.

Only this night their bud wasn't working, nor was his dad, the owner, who'd of known Abe and Lee.

Everyone there that night was a stranger.

Abe ordered Wellers and Coke and Lee started drinking a beer.

They sat at the bar.

Only a few moments passed by when a big arm reached past Abe with an empty beer pitcher and hammered it down on the bar by Abe's drink. The owner of the arm was as big and intimidating as his bicep. He asked for another pitcher. When he got it off the bar he suddenly looked at Abe and informed him in a slur, "Y'all ain't supposed to be in here. When I finish this beer," he stopped and lifted the pitcher like a mug to imply it was a single beer then continued, "I'm gonna come back and whip your ass if you're still here."

Abe didn't say anything as the biker took his beer by the handle and walked back to his table of buddies. The patch on his jacket indicated he was a Banshee.

Lee took Abe's lack of reply to the big fella to mean they would in fact not be there when he got back and suggested as much.

"Nah, we ain't leavin'," Abe said and drank more of his drink.

Lee left it at that but didn't feel great about the ass kicking he was about to take from a gang of Banshees. He finished his beer.

When he'd done so, Abe said, "Go get me the rabbit ears outta the truck." Abe knew Lee had a sawed off shotgun behind his truck seat.

Lee thought to protest then thought not to and amid indecision of how he felt about events unfolding he found himself at his truck in the parking lot retrieving the rabbit ears. He put shells in each barrel before putting the gun in the back of his jeans and letting his jacket fall over the round-ed stock.

Back inside he joined Abe at the bar again. He pushed his empty glass at the bar rail and leaned forward to expose the rounded stock of which Abe took hold, then pulled and placed the gun in his lap without moving from his bar stool.

Lee ordered another beer while Abe nursed his drink.

Sure enough, after he drank his pitcher of beer, the big Banshee came strolling back toward Abe and Lee swinging the empty pitcher like a lunch pail by its handle.

"So you gonna get goin'?" he asked as he reached the bar and slammed the empty pitcher down once again.

"No, we ain't botherin' no one," Abe replied calmly.

Lee looked at the big guy to see how'd he'd take the news.

"Well then, you wanna take an ass whoopin' I guess," the Banshee concluded with a tone of drunken logic in his voice. His gang at the table paid relatively little attention.

"No," Abe said and let it hang a second. Then he added, "We ain't leavin' and I ain't takin' an ass whoopin' to-night." He leaned back so the Banshee could see the double sawed-off hand held in his lap.

Lee was glad the other Banshees had paid no mind so far but he knew if the gun got picked up or someone swung they'd be in it quick. He positioned himself to be ready, whatever was coming.

"Where you from?" the big Banshee asked Abe sud-denly a bit more curious than threatening.

"We're from over at Madill. Just come over for a drink—get a little closer to the lake, smell that lake air. Don't reach to Madill. We went to school with the owner's son." Abe said all this in about the same tone with which the rest of the conversation had been delivered.

Lee was impressed with Abe's ability to talk to the biker like old men talking about the weather.

"Well—hell," the big Banshee said and grinned, "I was born over at the old hospital by the post office in Madill."

"No shit?" Lee said, hoping the grin and their being from the same place was going to make it friendly.

And it did. And Abe never lost his cool. They'd just been wrong place, wrong time, but Abe knew not to make a big deal. They wound up getting drunk with the big Banshee and his buddies that night.

Lee thought about that now. He knew his buddy Abe wouldn't do nothing dumb, but he wouldn't back down neither.

FRIDAY NIGHT

Abe didn't mention the Sledges or all that had happened, but enough folk had seen Abe and the Sledges in the diner's lot that Sara had already heard out at CW by closing time.

"I really wish you wouldn't be so reckless with these people." From Sara this really was a kind request.

"Was I going to NOT get King back?" was all Abe offered his second wife.

A little after nine, when King stood at the back door, Abe ignored him, figuring it best to keep him home for at least a night after everything.

When he went to bed, Abe dreamed about his son and the snake.

The dream was as clear as the memory.

Ike was three years old, the year before Abe and Agatha split. He was playing in the bar ditch on the Fourth Street side of the Dyson lot when he stepped, barefoot and dead-center, on a copperhead stretched out in the grass.

As Abe was coming into the house from the shop, he saw his frozen son in the bar ditch. He saw something was wrong.

Ike was dead still as the angry snake coiled his little leg in one snap motion, then inched up his leg toward his crotch.

Abe acted instinctively, racewalking across the yard toward his son in the ditch. Without breaking stride he stooped to pick up a shovel handle Ike must have dragged into the yard as a sword or baseball bat or some other plaything. As he approached the statue of his son Abe took a mighty swing and connected clean with the copperhead's arched-back head that was ready to strike. The snake's head flew across the road. His body uncoiled and fell limp at Ike's foot.

The first shot couldn't have been fired from anything more than a .22 pistol given the *pop* it made. Abe wouldn't have woken for it except that it had pierced the bathroom window and knocked a shelf of toiletries off the wall behind the bathroom door. It was 2:14 in the morning when he sat up.

Abe heard the next round of shots—*booms*—plain old multi-load buckshot. Much louder. Sara and the dog both woke at those.

Sara still hadn't formed words when Abe was on the move, telling her, "Stay down on the other side of the bed," and pulled his jeans on and stepped into his boots as he went out of the bedroom aiming to head to the backdoor, guessing correctly that the shots were being fired from the shop or back lot. He did though think to grab his .45 revolver and a box of shells from the gun cabinet in the spare room as quick as he could get the key in the lock. He passed through the house and was loaded by the time he swung off the carport toward his shop.

He caught another flash of pistol blast, the .22 again, in the corner of the lot by the impound fence's gate. He turned his march off the path he'd worn to the shop's door each day and moved cattycorner to the gate.

As he did so, he raised the gun and fired two shots into the persimmon tree branches that reached from the east edge of his property over the impound yard. Hot sticky leaves and fruit pulp and branch rained down on the two figures at the gate, who crouched and began to aim their guns all around, wildly searching for the shooter as Abe continued toward them in the dark. The figure to the right fired another shot from the pistol at the house.

"That was a goddamned hand cannon!" Abe heard Randy Sledge whisperyell to Andy just as he was close enough to see and hear the youngest Sledge boys. He was now within twenty-five feet or so.

"Is it Abe?" Andy asked.

"How the hell'd I know?" Randy snorted. They were both still crouching and bobbing and pointing their guns any which way trying to cover against their assaulter.

"I tol' you not to fire at the damned house," Randy said in a half cry, his voice breaking.

Abe was within a few steps and still unseen, but the Sledge boys could hear his movement.

"Where is that sombitch?"

No sooner than Randy had asked when Abe found himself at arm's length. Still in step, he pulled back his right arm in a big motion and hammered the Colt's butt down across Randy's nose and Randy dropped as suddenly as the dead snake's body had. After half a beat, the pain hit him, and Randy began spinning wildly on the gravel lot. As he did, Andy ran, barely hanging on to the black bag they'd brought and his pistol. He disappeared in the tree line that edged the property.

Abe kicked the long double-barrel shotgun Randy had dropped under the impound gate so it was inside the pin.

Randy clutched his face with both hands as he sat up and scampered to his knees so he was half standing, facing Abe Dyson.

"You sombitch," Randy managed to echo into the cupped hands across his face.

"Damn me—hitting an armed invader," Abe conceded and stooped to pick up another object on the ground he hadn't seen before.

"This a goddamned crossbow? What were y'all aimin' to do with this?" Abe asked, half laughing as he picked up the weapon.

"I don't know—it's Andy's," Randy managed as he stooped forward and then crawled up to standing from his knees.

"Must be a quite a pile of dope you're after—taking my dog, sneaking out here again," Abe offered, tossing the crossbow over the impound fence where it landed next to the shotgun. He looked down at the padlock on the impound gate. It had several small dents where Randy and Andy had blasted it with buckshot and the .22 pistol. It remained intact. "See you tried to bust the lock to boot."

"Whatcha mean?" Randy said, not responding to any specific accusation. Sledges came out coy. Never admitted to anything, not even in elementary school.

When Abe moved toward Randy he smelled whiskey. "Why you didn't think to just track down a pair of bolt cutters 'stead of assembling a little arsenal is what gets me."

Randy Sledge wasn't paying attention, was simply holding his bloody nose, head tilted back, and waited for Abe to be done before asking all he cared about: "You gonna call the cops on me, Abe Dyson?"

Abe thought honestly for a moment. Calling the cops hadn't occurred to him. Then he replied, "Nah—you didn't do anything besides scuff my lock and break a window. I known drunks to do way worse." Abe didn't want to escalate the fight though assured, "Could be the other end of the.45 next time though."

"Alright, Abe," Randy said beat, managing to keep only a single eye open.

"Git on," Abe said, and walked toward the shop office to grab a cigarette. As he entered the side door, Randy crossed the northeast corner of the lot and walkran toward the highway holding his busted gourd all the while. Abe grabbed a cigarette from an open pack on his desk and lit it with a match from a box in the drawer. He closed the shop office door behind him and made his way to the house with his cigarette.

Sara met him at the porch with some panic, "A bullet went through Ike's window. Lodged right in the headboard."

This hit Abe awkwardly. He just thought of it as a

bedroom, hardly Ike's room. Abe's son hadn't lived there since the divorce. He'd only stayed there a few weeks of a few summers. Though Sara was right—it's where Ike would have been if he'd been there. "Damn," Abe managed.

After Sara was back asleep and Abe had laid there restlessly for an hour or more, he crawled back out of bed still wearing his jeans from before. He put his boots back on in the kitchen, went back out the back, and crossed the lot toward the impound pin, now in the just-daylight.

He unlocked the scuffed padlock using the ring of keys from his pocket and loosed the chain from around the right cyclone gate door before pushing it open as he moved toward the Sledges' impounded truck.

The camper on the truck's bed was unlocked. Abe lifted it, stepped up on the bumper, and dove into his waist grabbing the back edge of the big cardboard box with the dog food. He slid the box back to the tailgate by dropping down off the bumper without letting go of the box.

He let down the tailgate to give his five foot eight inch frame a better look. After a brief pause he reached into the dog food with both arms and began to sift around. He'd reached near to the bottom before he found it. Both hands stopped, blocked hard by a bigger, solid object. He grabbed and pulled the object. A briefcase surfaced from the dog food.

Abe tried to imagine who around here would carry a briefcase. Bankers, a couple of accountants, and lawyers at the courthouse, where Abe suspected the Sledges would have lifted this one.

He debated opening it when he saw a little metal plate engraved with "CW Trailer Mfg." on the case lid's right front corner.

Abe took the case into the shop's office, leaving the truck camper and tailgate open and the shotgun and cross-bow laying in the gravel. He remembered to wrap the chain and snap the lock shut on the gate.

In his office, he pulled another cigarette and lit it and looked at the case and thought about welding. Abe welded livestock trailers before he opened the shop. He worked for Canaan Wheeler ten or twelve years before he'd spent a few years at the tire plant in Ardmore. Eventually he had enough working for others and opened his own branch of the family business.

He knew the companyman this case belonged to.

He hoped what he had was not what he had, but knew better. He put the cigarette into an upside down pis-ton head he used as an ashtray, balancing it on the edge. Abe grabbed the case and unsnapped both latches and let the case lid open.

Paperwork and checks sat there in a heap. Some cash too. Personal files and finances for Jim Canaan, son of the cofounder of Canaan Wheeler Trailers, Big Jim Canaan. Lit-tle Jim shortened the company name to "CW Trailer Manu-facturing" when he bought the old men out and shoved them both off. That was two or three years after Abe quit welding there.

Visions of events of the summer prior flashed. Lit-tle Jim and his wife built a big house out on the lake. A compound really. Last summer, while they were on vacation, someone emulexed the electronic gate, torched the room around the fireproof safe Jim had buried in the wall in the middle of the house, loaded the safe from the charred ruins of the house up on one of Jim's trucks from the garage, and drove off.

Sara worked in the supply warehouse as inventory quality control for CW. She'd heard all the theories in gossip at work. Abe could've guessed them before she even told it.

Angry workers was the first thought. Little Jim didn't give vacation. Instead, he shut down the whole operation for two weeks in the summer, and paid everyone for a week off. Anytime someone tried to take time during the year, he'd scoff, reminding them they got two whole weeks in the summer. It was natural to think then that resentful employees wanted to punish the boss, knowing he was on vacation, somewhere they couldn't afford to go, and so terrorized his property and split the proceeds.

Problem was, everything was too professional and precise and accurate. Emulex on the gate would have needed procurement. Sara and Abe couldn't imagine anyone on the CW staff with that kind of connection save a couple. Add beating the security alarm, knowing the safe was fireproof and in the wall, knowing how to bypass the electronic pad on the garage and wire the truck, that seemed like an electronics and metal and explosives expert. A few folks met that description around town, Lee Pitchman included, though he was with Abe the day it happened and wasn't never so criminal anyway.

Local cops didn't go out of their way to work the case for Jim Canaan. They came to the quick conclusion that it was an inside job, probably a conman on the alarm install crew or the safe install crew. The tone of the conclusion came with the hint that Little Jim Canaan got what he deserved for having so much nice stuff and coveting it so much and needing so many security measures to begin with.

Abe thought that was a reasonable conclusion at the time. When Little Jim's truck had been found with the blown safe underwater a few months later by a boater near the center of the bridge that crossed Lake Texoma into Texas at Willis Point, it did nothing to confirm or deny the theory.

All that talk and lack of investigation and conclusions and accusations and the answer was really the simplest. The Sledges done it.

Oakland sprung up first—built a school for Indians and whites, built a store, a hotel, landed a post office. This was the 1870s after some old Confederate army officer built a house in the middle of an oak grove and put a couple thousand head of cattle on the property. A few years passed and on a backdoor swindle the little community of Madill, two miles southeast of the booming town of Oakland, won the train station and track that come with it. Subsequent, the county seat moved and Madill got a courthouse and a new post office and all else while Oakland stagnated and eventually consolidated its school and post office to throw in with Madill's much better lot. This was all still Chickasaw Nation territory.

As the territory became state and roads became highways, State Highway70 was built, bisecting Oakland and running west to east parallel to the Red River, which was some seventeen miles south. Highway 70 runs east from Oakland to the north end of Madill, now the county seat of what was christened Marshall County, the smallest county in all of Oklahoma. Highway 70 T's with US Highway 377 there at the north end of Madill and 377 runs south with Madill trickling along either side of it.

There is an insurance office and an old rundown motel at the north end of Madill, then going south on either side of 377 is a Sonic drive-in, Allen's Pawn, Hobo Joe's diner of course, the old drive-through pharmacy converted by Byron Salt to Byron's Bail Bonds, an intersection with the courthouse to the east and old post office to the west, the Pitt BBQ, a tire shop, Tequila's Mexican Restaurant, an abandoned grocery store, a Love's station, a Sinclair station, a china buffet in what used to be a KFC, and then the Y intersection where 70 splits off again and curves southeast out of town toward the littler town of Kingston on the way to the lake and the bigger city of Durant. The newest Madill enterprises have built up of late along this stretch including a couple of new autoparts stores, an Indian smokeshop and casino, a new motel, and the new Wal-Mart. Oklahoma Steel & Wire anchors the southeastest Madill city limit out that way and has for years. Meanwhile back at the Y-intersect, Highway 377curves and meanders a few miles west past a nursing home complex, a daycare center, the hospital, and CW Manufacturing before a big bend south and the southwestest Madill city limit. Oakland, Madill, and the bend of 377 south form a neat triangle, about four or five miles on each side. The bottom points south to Lake Texoma, about seventeen miles down Highway 377, and the north Texas pastures beyond the lake toward Whitesboro, a town about thirty miles south of the 377 bend.

This is the heart of Texoma.

The Dysons come to town when Abe was nine or ten. His uncle, JL Dyson, had gotten a job as a body man and shop manager at the Chevrolet House after plane building and repair during the Korean War. JL invited his older brother, Abe's daddy, OE Dyson, down as mechanic given OE's experience as Army mechanic and landing craft driver in World War II and his need for a new job and fresh start for his young family.

OE, always called "Shorty" on account of his five foot four inch stature, took a Veteran's loan and slowly paid for the little Oakland lot, west of Madill where he enjoyed work not only in the Chevy House, but as volunteer sheriff's deputy as well. Volunteer sheriff wasn't a post that offered a lot of extra income, but it offered a kind of excitement without a lot of commitment or serious stakes for a World War II veteran with an itch for just that.

Before Oakland and Madill, OE Dyson had moved his family around Oklahoma, Missouri, where Abe was born, Colorado, and Oklahoma again. He'd chased one job opportunity after the other resisting his family's farm life in Dewey County in Northern Oklahoma where OE and JL and their siblings had weathered the Dust Bowl with their folks on forty acres.

Young Abe Dyson had thought the Oakland house and property and the Madill School as the next stop on what had been a pretty continuous transient life at that point. He'd never really had friends or steady family besides his folks with all the moving. Madill was the sixth school he'd seen by the fourth grade.

After a few years there though it was home, and Abe didn't want to move again. And really hadn't.

When Abe got engaged to Agatha, Ike's mother, OE gave his son the back side of the double lot to put a trailer on and eventually build his own house, which he'd done. A few years on after that and despite his younger ambitions, OE Shorty Dyson retired to the family's forty acres in Northern Oklahoma, leaving Abe the whole lot to tend.

As Abe looks through the contents of the case, it is

clear it is something valuable. He sees maps and surveys, memos and plans. They indicate a highway expansion of sorts. A residential road already connects Highway 70 from Oakland just east of the Oakland Grocery to 377 before the big bend south, though, as it exists, is hardly a bypass for Madill, with its narrow pavement and several stop signs. Not to mention all the houses that pock its path whose many residents may pull out of a driveway or meander from the curbless yards into the road. As Abe examined everything it was clear that Little Jim Canaan had developed a plan to build a new byway from 70 to the 377 bend south that would create a new business vein for the western edge of Madill. Not to mention eat up Oakland pretty well in full. Abe's lot sat pretty near a new designated intersection with a flashing light. The new byway would be "Business 70" and run down the rural residential road while widening it.

A detailed memo outlined the basic points, highlighting enticement for city participation. First, Madill owned a good chunk of the land itself already. Between the City Lake Park, the water maintenance facility and its acreage, and two historic homes, all within a block or so of the current route, Madill could easily makes its case for further eminent domain. Second, a case could be made for the faster route to the hospital of current citizens of Oakland—despite the fact that many would be displaced by the north end of the new route—and the folks from northwest rural parts of the county.

Three major blocks existed as far as could be seen for Little Jim Canaan's plot, of which it was clear would benefit him greatly by placing a new major intersection and route to his CW Manufacturing at the southwest corner of Madill. There was the Logan Bird ranch holdings which ate up a good chunk of the south end of the proposed route. Logan was a retired dentist whose old dentistry sat vacant west of the post office in town. On the southeast end of Oakland toward the north end of the proposed route was quite a collection of trailers owned and inhabited primarily by a mixture of legal and illegal Mexican families who found gainful employment regardless of status as local ranch hands or as welders at one of the several steel and trailer manufacturing companies around the county, including CW. Then there was Sonny Howe's widow's holdings which included several rental properties along the route.

Abe's lot was in the way as well—the turn lanes and signage of the new intersection would need the block up to and including Abe's off the highway—but was not cited specifically in the memo.

The largest enticement the memo outlined last, which was of course that this provided a faster route from the larger city of Ardmore thirty miles west of Oakland in the next county and rural folks more north to the new businesses on the south end of Madill and the Lake. That also of course meant even more new opportunity for business. The city park could be converted to a rest and picnic area with vending machines. There would be a need for more gas stations. The historic homes could be marketed to tourists driving in that might be enticed off the nearest interstate sooner by the new faster vein to the lake.

It was all a good plan as far as Abe could tell except that it didn't look like it included him keeping his property or business. Or leaving much of Oakland for Oakland.

A pocket ledger at the bottom of the case looked intriguing and Abe found its contents more shady. It outlined specific payments. Certain politicians and beaurocrats of otherwise unworthy note. More tidy sums were proffered to be paid to higher level state politicians that even Abe had heard of though he cared little for politics on any level. Even more tidy sums were documented to be paid to already selected companies for building, of which CW represented a very large shareholding. CW Manufacturing would provide all metal building materials of course.

The ledgerbook was enough to show it wasn't all on the up.

Little Jim Canaan could build an empire with it if it went through.

At some point, as he sifted through the case, Abe felt the need to dump it. Not the contents necessarily. Not the information. He damn sure needed that, even if he had figured by now the reason the Sledges was coming so hard for it was they figured Little Jim would pay a handsome sum to them not to have the information out of his control. He needed the originals probably too so it couldn't be charged nothing was forged.

Abe resolved the briefcase itself needed to be thrown off. How he got the information needed to be gotten rid of. If he was found to have the case at some point, it could be argued against him he stole it directly. Maybe even he'd be linked to the robbery and arson of the Canaan mansion the summer before.

And goddamned if Abe Dyson didn't just feel the need to throw something off. Shit was feeling heavy. He lit and smoked another cigarette.

Little Jim'd be in Mexico now. It was where he always went, shutting the company down for its annual mandatory and un-flexible vacation centered around a timeshare of the Canaan family. It was why Sara'd be able to go to the family wedding in New Mexico. It happened to fall during the CW shutdown, though she and other CW employees had missed many a family wedding or graduation or funeral over the years on account of Little Jim only allowed the mandatory shut down for paid personal days.

Abe and Lee had both started out welding horse trailers at CW right out of high school. Big Jim and Mr. Wheeler had liked both boys. Abe mostly liked working for CW then. He welded and hauled trailers all over the region. Agatha had pushed him though to move over to the tire plant at Ardmore for the better pay and benefits and he did so when Ike came along. Abe'd worked there about as long as he could stand it before opening his shop with a loan against the lot.

Outside the little appleknocker town of Cobden, IL hidden in the hills of the Shawnee Forest between the confluence of the Ohio and Mississippi Rivers, a screen door slams shut. Ike Dyson is packed and headed for his daddy's lot. He can't figure any place else to go.

BUNCOMBE CREEK SHOOTOUT

SATURDAY

The loose asphalt roads of Oakland, Oklahoma are in a constant negotiation of boundary with the grassy storm ditches because there are no curbs. Ike realizes as he drives back into town that the place never had curbs. It hadn't been anything he'd notice running around as a kid. Now that he'd been in a world of curbs for a few years, he really noticed it, couldn't not. It wobbled his field of vision.

It's early in the morning. The sun has only been up a bit, but it has refreshed Ike Dyson some. He'd been driving just eleven hours, from Illinois, but had decided to make the trip at night in the dark so time passed quicker. If he had to watch the sun move across the sky and the daylight change colors while sitting in the driver's seat the whole time with interstate in front of him, it'd make time drag. If he left after dark and it just stayed dark the whole time, it wouldn't feel like so much of a piece of a time had passed.

Now that he is pulling in he wonders why making time or how time passed should matter at all. It was all just a habit of so many hours on so many roads. He wasn't really in a hurry or trying to save time now. In fact, lately it felt he'd just been eating time. The last couple years or a little more. He was full of it.

He didn't have anything particular to get to either. He had a little teachings stipend money left from the school year and no real plan for the next year, other than he wouldn't be going back to where he was coming from. Ike looked in his rearview mirror: his Jeep Wagoneer was littered with his few possessions but by no means packed full. He didn't really have a reason for coming back to Oakland or his dad's lot, other than he didn't know where he wanted to go next.

He'd only vaguely let his folks know he'd back some-time soon. Then, when he finally got the energy up for driv-ing, he'd let 'em know about the day he'd be in. He hadn't talked to his dad about it. Sara had answered when he called and he talked to her.

He never gave a time or a reason for coming or how long he might be staying. There was no time then that he needed to be there. Still, as soon as he'd come in to Oakland and made a couple of turns, he was at his dad's lot.

Abe woke in his recliner. He'd only shut his eyes an hour or so before, though some rest felt better than none. He'd stayed up all night and saw Sara off a couple hours after first light when she left to pick up her sister then head to New Mexico for the wedding. He'd sat out in the shop's office for a bit with the briefcase. Then he'd come in and flipped chan-nels in the recliner until Sara woke.

Now he stirred, used the bathroom, started coffee, lit his first cigarette of the day. He had a slight headache. Stress and not a lot of sleep most likely. Maybe he'd sucked too much gunpowder in the exchange the night before. Damned Sledges.

It wasn't the worst he'd hurt. He'd certainly been hit out of the blue before.

Abe'd been working welding horse trailers right out of high school. Soon as he was eighteen, he'd started rodeoing on the side as well.

One Thursday night Abe was at the bar at Durant after the rodeo and knew he couldn't stay long on account of he had to work the next morning. He had a couple of Wellers and Cokes and told everyone he was headed out.

A couple of girls he'd gone to high school with were stranded at the bar and looking for a ride and asked Abe to haul 'em back to Madill.

Abe said 'of course' and didn't think nothing of it.

Apparently the girls had been getting harassed all night by a drunk cowboy out of Broken Bow and were glad to leave with Abe. The drunk cowboy wasn't so glad and got it into his head that Abe was running off with his girls.

Well Abe went to crawl into the cab of his pickup when he was thudded with a beer bottle. Before he could turn around again the drunk cowboy hammered the bottle down again, smashing it against the back of Abe's head and lodging cut-up glass and cuts all in Abe's new silverbelly hat.

Abe was staggered and stunned but didn't collapse.

He leaned forward into the open cab resting his gut against the edge of the pickup's bench seat.

Before the inebriate could get any more hits in, Lee and one of his and Abe's rodeo buddies, Scooter Frazier, who'd watched the drunk cowboy angrily amble after Abe and the girls and followed in case, grabbed the attacker and pulled him backwards down into the gravel lot and pinned him.

Abe came to his senses enough to reach and grab the big hunting knife from his dash. The two girls didn't scream out but gasped and huddled by the back of the truck.

Abe was pissed and unsheathed the knife and whirled and lunged toward the cowboy on the ground. There was little thought to what was next. Abe looked like an angry bobcat with a car bearing down on him.

Abe's buddies saw this and knew he might get himself in trouble.

Scooter stopped him and advised, "Get these ladies out of here Abe."

Abe realized his new fine silverbelly was ruined as he felt the cuts in the back of his beer soaked hat. But he knew better than to let a drunk goad him into criminal offence. Folks had started to gather in the lot. He dropped the knife to his side and eased off the balls of his feet to his heels.

"Go on—get in the cab," Scooter said and nodded at the girls who complied.

Abe did likewise, throwing the knife and the sheath back on the dash and crawled under the wheel. He shook his head to steady his senses. He left the hat on his head not wanting to let glass and blood loose in the truck cab. He turned the key and started the truck.

Abe's buddies had no trouble holding the drunk cowboy down while Abe dusted the parking lot and pulled on the highway back toward Madill.

In the end, Abe'd only been mildly concussed and the cowboy hat had saved his head from cuts bad enough to need stitching. He only needed to wash and take care when he got home.

There was no salvaging the silverbelly.

The next weekend Abe hadn't put his entry in in-time so was not riding, only scouting, at the Pauls Valley Rodeo. He was particularly interested in a bull he'd rode at Durant the week before for 7.9 seconds—J-22 Leapin' Lizard, a big white Limousin bull that felt like riding a concrete slab. Abe figured watching Leapin' Lizard throw a few other cowboys he might see something to help get him over on the next ride.

Abe never made it into the Pauls Valley stands to watch. As he went behind the chutes to say 'hey' to a few buddies he seen the drunk cowboy from the weekend before. The cowboy wasn't drunk now but had clearly been drunk enough then that he didn't recognize Abe at all.

Abe boiled but didn't let on. He said 'hey' to his buddies and walked back to his truck.

He reached in the bed of the pickup and opened the ice chest. He grabbed a Coke bottle and let the lid close. He walked back to the chutes and waited for the cowboy to turn around. He wasn't going to hit the old boy from behind same as he was done.

When the cowboy turned around Abe swung the un-opened Coke bottle and busted him across the bridge of his nose. There was a loud thud. The thick green glass coke bottle hadn't shattered like the beer bottle had.

The cowboy collapsed unconscious.

Scooter Frazier was the only one that seen the whole thing go down. The cowboy probably hadn't even gotten a good look at Abe before he was knocked out. Scooter went and ushered Abe out of the chute area and out to the horse trailers where the early riders were already drinking rodeo warm beer before anyone saw anything and Abe got himself in trouble.

Scooter and Abe didn't mention it again, even when commotion arose in the chute area that a cowboy was knocked out behind the pins. They just kept drinking their beer. There wasn't need to do anything. Abe never spoke on it. Certainly never bragged on it. Abe considered the matter finished.

The cowboy that was knocked out didn't show up much on the Southern Oklahoma circuit again, maybe not at all.

In the driveway of the Dyson lot, Ike crawls out of his Jeep, the door popping hinge rust loose loudly when he shuts it. His dad is in the open carport drinking coffee, where he's been watching the dog sniff around the yard. Abe is struck by how skinny Ike has grown. Abe must show this as Ike suddenly looks as if he feels embarrassed.

"You're too damned skinny," Abe offers, trying to be jovial about it.

"Oh-yea," Ike manages in reply, having grown used to this frame over the past several years. He'd always been chubby. He'd gotten fat after high school and he was no longer playing ball and was partying at college. He shaved it all quickly one summer on too much speed and opioids and made up a story about a running regimen and now folks usually told him, if they commented at all, he seemed too skinny, especially people he saw that used to be skinny but had grown older and fatter themselves.

Abe changed the subject for him. As usual, Abe steered the conversation toward cars. "Pretty straight bodied old Jeep you're drivin' there," he said. "Sounds good too," he added.

"Oh yea," Ike said, picking up his old rhythm with his dad. "Picked it up a couple years ago around Rockford, IL. Only cost me a couple of water pumps and the cost of maintenance so far."

An hour in and Ike is smoking hand-rolled cigarettes constantly, ashes piling on his leg and the worn arm of the reclining rocker he is in.

"When'd you switch to those?" Abe asks his son, recalling a period of occasional menthol smoking by Ike when he was in college.

"Few years now. Always liked 'em when Lee'd would let me bum one."

Abe was struck by the way Ike had called Wild Child, "Lee," though that was his name. He realized he'd never wondered what bad habits Ike mighta picked up around him. Always seemed it wouldn't be much as his son did most of his growing up on the other side of the lake, with his mom and stepdad. "Roll me one," he says to his son in a gruff command of affection.

"Yea," Ike says and goes to it. "Here," Ike says when Abe lands on *El Dorado* on TV, and Abe obliges. They both smoke hand-rolled cigarettes and watch John Wayne and Robert Mitchum and James Caan.

As they watch and smoke, Abe glances toward Ike. He finds it somehow strangely satisfying that Wild Child should influence Ike still though Ike'd been gone so long. Ike was also still thinking on Lee Pitchman.

Ike put two J-hooks on U-bolts attached to a chain under the front A-frames of the Mercury and hooked the I-hooks attached to the U-bolts at the other end of the chain into T-slots on the back of Stinky Foot's bumper, which Lee had now backed in front of the rusty car.

The Mercury looked liked it'd been driven into the side of the red dirt hill at ninety miles an hour and hadn't stopped 'til she was stuck to the back windows. Stinky Foot, Lee's custom-built truck, has a winch on the front bumper, but the cable is rusted, seems ready to snap any minute, and has for years. The cable creaked and groaned, pulled the nose of the '54 Ford hard against its Blazer frame and suspension. The groans of the cable echoed across the top of the Oklahoma pasture and bounced through the pecan tree orchards as Lee winched the Mercury slowly out.

Ike's dad's bud Lee Pitchman was always grabbin' Ike outta bed for shit like this.

The Mercury eased back from the half-hill its nose was submerged in. Ike wondered how in the hell a car like that got stuck in a hill like this.

The burgundy-rust-colored car was surprisingly complete. Shitty, but still a whole car.

We got a trailer? Ike asked.

We got a chain. You can drive, right? Lee asked in reply.

Drive what where?

Brakes are still good on the Mercury, so we're going to pull it back to your Dad's shop.

Okay.

The car was officially out once Lee had pulled it even further away and more perpendicular to the way it was against the hill by easing backwards in Stinky Foot and creaking the cable some more. Ike got it pretty well by that point. He, the twelve year old, was either driving a '54 Ford lifted with an '85 Blazer suspension draggin' an '84 Mercury down Oklahoma highway, or he was being pulled in the Mercury, hoping the brakes held at every stop and turn.

Ike was damned excited.

Lee had Ike remove the chain from the cable and draw the winch back up. Then Lee crawled into Stinkyfoot again. He wheeled the truck around so its back was to the Mercury's front now. Lee had Ike reattach the chain to another chain which Lee attached to his truck's back bumper.

Ike had the windows rolled down, with great effort against the dirt and God knows what else shit was in the glass and brackets and regulators of the rusty car. The tandem was moving at about forty-three miles an hour according to the median position of the bouncing speedometer on the rolling Mercury.

The brakes were surprisingly stiff. This was good because the unaccounted hazard of hot Oklahoma wind inside a Pecan-sapped and mildewy Mercury concocted to blow what seemed like host mustard gas down Ike's eyes and nose and throat. Ike adjusted as best as could after a few miles, and they were halfway home to the shop, no problems so far.

Ike stuck his elbow on the little remaining top of the window that wouldn't quite roll all the way down and put his right hand at the top of the wheel. He didn't know what they were going to do with the car when they got it to the shop, but he was excited to find out.

The tandem rambled on down the Oklahoma highway.

Turned out Lee wanted Ike to help him rip the rear-end out from under the car and use it for the axle of trailer he was building. They scrapped the rest of the Mercury at Buddy's Crushed Cars.

At one point during the movie, Ike rises and heads across the dingy, worn living room carpet and down the hallway to the bathroom. Abe does not seem to regard this and is stretched back in his chair with his eyes on the TV. King sleeps on the floor at the foot of Abe's chair.

When Ike closes the door he tries to nonchalantly and silently click the lock as well only to find its spring busted and the knob loosely attached to begin with. The worn carpet's edge pushed over the threshold and combined with the shitty knob prevented the door from latching shut, let alone locking. Ike held his foot against the bottom of the door and pulled pills from his jeans pocket.

His forehead had begun to sweat a bit but the cigarettes and coffee had kept him buzzed enough in the interim. He downed five of the white pills from the little container in his pocket, using his cupped hand to get water from the faucet though his stepmom had stocked the bathroom with little Dixie cups.

He flushed and immediately realized he should have done so before turning on the faucet. He pulled the loose door open and switched out the light and walked back into the living room to find Abe still watching in his chair and Robert Mitchum sitting in a bathtub.

As the movie played Ike hoped his dad was going to

save any questions about why he was back. Ten or fifteen minutes from the end of the movie Ike looked over to see Abe sleeping.

It was coming up on late morning.

Ike looked down at his hiking boots and noted again the burn marks on the right toes. He stood up, and went into his old room.

Sara had hung some of her tribal art here. Otherwise, the spare room had the combined antiques of Abe and Sara's folks. An old Zenith TV, a brass bed, a closet full of old clothes--Ike's grandmother's, papa's, and dad's old wears.

A smell of leather and sweet damp and paint hit Ike as he opened the closet door. There was a line of tan and blue paint by the door jamb. Sara had painted over his mom's Robin's egg blue over the years. This room was tan and khaki now. Only the dingy bathroom had Ike's mom's original colors left.

Ike began to leaf through the hanging clothes. He stopped at Abe's denim jacket. It was his dad's during high school. On the back was stitched, in home-sewn letters by Abe's mom, "Ike" in small pink font under the seam across the back of the right upper shoulder. "Ike" had been an inside joke--something Abe's best buddies called him for a time in school and after.

Abe's mom had no idea why her son had her sew it on his jacket. Abe's dad, OE, knew full well. Of course, it was how Ike would come by his name. It became a high school nickname for Abe on account of a prank his dad's dad, OE, played. Ike had heard the story too.

OE "Shorty" Dyson was a laugher—laughed and

smiled to the point he had smile lines when he was old were most around that hard country would have frown and scowl lines. When there was nothing to make Shorty laugh, he'd sure make himself smile.

In the '52 election, the year Abe'd been born, a local Madill screen printer went a little nuts seeing what all he could stick a "Like Ike" logo on during the presidential campaign. Coffee cups, t-shirts, stickers—he printed all the standard fare first. Then he did baseball bats and pie tins, swept up with putting "Ike" on all things Americana. The print ink failed to stick to the pie tin long and he soon gave up on branding any more Americana and turned his attention to the humorous: Men's boxer shorts and lady's panties were stamped "Like Ike" in various and salacious positions on the underpants.

Somehow in there, a surplus box of the printer's Ike-underwear wound up in the back of the warehouse at the city Chevy lot where Shorty Dyson was mechanic. Shorty found them sometime in the early sixties and got a particularly big grin out of the panties.

When his son was a teenager in the late sixties, he was in the shop one day telling Shorty he had a date.

Shorty got an idea for another smile and grabbed a pair of the Ike panties and stashed them in his son's car when Abe wasn't looking, he placed them in the crevice of the bench seat on the passenger side near the passenger buckle. He hoped Abe's date would find them and think Abe was fooling with another girl before her. That would be funny.

Abe's date did happen to find the Ike panties. She did happen to believe they must belong to some other girl and she did get pissed at Abe. Shorty Dyson laughed like mad when his son came home early and pissy himself. Shorty made sure Abe's buddies knew about it when they come around. "Like Ike" was often uttered with a grin as an inside joke from Abe's buddies and pretty soon "Ike" was Abe's occasional nickname. It never stuck like "Shorty," and by the time Abe was out of school a few years the nickname was pretty well dropped.

Agatha, Ike's mom, never quite knew the full story, just that Abe's old friends called him "Ike" and liked the thought of naming her son after his father in some way at the time. And she did think of Abraham and Isaac from the Bible. In fact, she put "Isaac" on Ike's birth certificate, though he'd never be called that, because she felt it was classier on the official document. Later she wished she'd named him "Pernell," after her favorite actor, Pernell Roberts.

Under the hanging bar of clothes on the closet floor were a few carefully collected pairs of shoes and boots.

Abe's mother's orthopedic Velcro shoes were buried on the far left--they meant nothing, Abe simply neglected to throw them out after his mom passed. A pair of moccasins that belonged to Sara's dad, a gift from Navajos when he principaled a reservation school in New Mexico, rested next to the old lady shoes. The pair of women's laceup boots, small sized, were a mystery to Ike. To the right of the women's boots were OE's dark brown roper boots. He'd worn them with his volunteer sheriff's uniform--brown and khaki colored.

Ike bent over and picked up his grandfather's boots and backed to and sat on the edge of the brass bed in the room. He pulled back the collar of the right boot. They were tens, a size smaller than Ike normally wore, a half size bigger than what Abe wore.

In a mood, Ike decided to pull them on anyway and kicked off his laceup chukkas. He pulled the old ropers on and pulled his jeans down over the boots and stood. His ankle turned and he tripped a little though he recovered. They fit perfect.

He closed the closet door, scooted his discarded chukkas under the bed, and switched off the light as he went back out into the living room.

His ears had a comforting dull roar and his temples felt stroked. The pills were still the good ones, not the government ordered formula shit you had to snort or smoke to get buzzed like this.

"Hey," Abe was awake and rolling a cigarette on his own from Ike's cheap tobacco pouch. "I ain't even gonna ask how you got so good at this rollin'," Abe joked before he licked and twisted the cigarette paper. It rained cherry ashes into the chair as he lit the sloppier end and the excess tobacco burned off.

"Then I ain't sayin'," Ike said, and took the bag from the side table between his and Abe's chairs and rolled his own smoke. "Sara check in at all?" he asked once it was lit.

"Not 'chet. Just a long boring drive to New Mexico."

"I imagine so," Ike said, though the notion seemed quite nice. As he spoke, he crossed his feet out in front of the chair and leaned back. Abe looked down and saw his dad's boots on his son's feet.

Ike noticed Abe notice and nodded at the boots and asked, "That ok?"

"Yea--of course," Abe said without thinking but decided he meant it once he did. "You wanna go get a bite to eat?"

Ike wasn't hungry. Pills kept it that way most of the time, different than when he smoked weed. He figured though he could take on coffee and part of a sandwich. "Hobo Joe's?" he asked not really asking but knowing, to which Abe nodded. "Let me just use the bathroom," Ike said.

This time, Ike flushed then turned the tap to swallow his pills. His body hummed and swelled and felt good about everything without thinking about anything specifically.

As he rode shotgun in Abe's Bronco Ike wondered if this would be so easy sober. Highway 70, Oakland Grocery, the turn into Madill, the Sonic, where the Burger Hut used to be, Hobo Joe's limestone gravel parking lot radiating this hot Oklahoma sun in waves. None of it was alien, foreign, or strange, the way Ike imagined coming back would be all those miles and nights away. Everything seemed like he'd just been here the whole time even if there were a few new things here or there.

"Can we go to the Post Office?" Ike's question caught Abe off guard. He'd already killed the engine in the diner parking lot, the same he'd come barreling into the day before. Not that that was odd as Hobo Joe's Diner was where he went to eat if he went to town to eat.

"Now?"

"After we eat maybe," Ike offered.

"Why?"

"There's just that old painting, that mural in there. I always liked it. Wanted to see it again. Still there?"

Abe had never thought twice about the western scene on the lobby wall of the post office but now imagined it well for he'd seen it a thousand times or more. "Yea, sure," he said.

The Dyson boys went into the diner.

By the time Ike's eyes adjusted from the bright sun and the flash spots and vibes danced out of his vision, Abe was already making his way to a six-top corner table where Jack Peavine and Jerry Dye were already seated, shooting the shit.

"Hey, hey--you got the bossman with you today," Jack Peavine said warmly, just as he had when Ike was a kid. He too was exactly as Ike remembered him--a full head of snow white hair, a clean shave, smiling blue eyes that were softer'n most men around here, stocky like Abe, a black t-shirt, jeans, and motorcycle boots. "How the hell old are you now? Or do I want to know?" Jack Peavine asked Ike with a wink without winking.

"Twenty-nine."

"Well shit, it has been a minute," Jerry Dye chimed in.

Jerry Dye too was unchanged. Big ears under his cap, pointy nose, big glasses, no chin, a pearl snap faded paisley shirt, jeans with his legs crossed sharply, vertically, like a woman in a skirt, and a cigarette burning in his boney right hand. He'd turned his chair so he awkwardly held the corner of the head of the table.

"It has," Ike agreed.

Jerry Dye was missing a good portion of his penis and most folks know the story why. Ike didn't just know. He seen it. As they seated themselves on the empty side of the table, Ike thought about Jerry Dye's penis.

When he saw him, Ike wished he hadn't come back this way. But the fat was in the fire now and Ike didn't imagine he could leave the guy alone much as he didn't want to worry about nothing or no one else.

The day was broilin' hot and the Texoma sun, humid air, and dried brown grass wrapped Ike like a blanket of warm urine.

Ike was languid wondering where the energy to even bike the rest of the way to his dad's lot would come when he saw Jerry Dye up against his garage—spectral and wan. Ike first figures it's the heat but the juice of red down Jerry's right leg flowing from his groin says it ain't just that.

Though a tad Ike knew women bleed. And their waters break. And babies come out bloody. For a moment Ike thought Jerry Dye must be a woman.

Jerry sees his buddy's young son and rambles at him while Ike wonders where Jerry has all this energy havin' just given birth. Jerry Dye talks broken and breathless. *There was a circular saw and a shopvac attached for saw dust and the board was just restin' across his thigh and he just needed to shave a little and he must not a paid attention because he's pretty sure he's cut part of it off and it musta sucked up in the shopvac if it's still intact anyways.*

Fortunately Ike don't have to utter a word. Jerry directs Ike to *living room… phone next to chair…call the ambulance.* Ike Dyson is still tryin' to figure a way to just keep goin' back to his dad's house. He stays here in the summer and folks like Jerry Dye come in and out of his world. Rather, he drifts in and out of theirs. He remembers names and faces and occasionally the right face with the right name. He's always surprised when they know who he is.

The heat makes everything seem outterbody and Ike feels himself slip and scramble and stumble into the house. Jerry Dye's bachelor pad smells sweet and smoky. Ike sees himself dial. Hears himself talk to the 911 operator.

A man is hurt in his driveway is the best Ike can offer. He cannot name the address. He don't live here all the time. He's visitin' his daddy for the summer.

Well who are you? comes back through the line and Ike is dumb.

He searches and scans and racks his brain and damned if he can figure a way to answer while Jerry Dye continues to bleed.

Of course 911 traced the call and the ambulance drivers stemmed the bleeding and the doctors sewed his wound without reattachment of the missing end.

Folks call Jerry "Hoover" since that episode and Ike would feel worse for him if he didn't seem like a little bit of a dick otherwise. Ike always feels a little uncomfortable around Jerry.

Jerry works on computers, whatever that means in Madill, Oklahoma. He was trained at Uniroyal in Ardmore as a computer tech when Abe had worked there cutting rubber. At some point he took his computer training and set up shop in town, working out of his house setting up and repairing computers for local businesses. He did pretty well from what Ike always understood.

Ike was starting to want coffee. He figured he'd humor everyone by ordering a plain turkey sandwich though he still didn't intend to eat much. He never opened the menu the waitress had brought. Abe hadn't even been brought a menu. He knew the menu backwards and forwards and never ventured beyond biscuits and gravy at breakfast or a patty melt otherwise.

Lola, a middle-aged blonde with the cuffs of her jean shorts rolled, brought the order and kept their coffee full. Abe and Ike both left half of their sandwiches or more on the plate.

After insisting on to-go boxes only to be brushed back by the Dyson boys, Lola took their plates away. As she walked from the table back to the kitchen, Clifford Blow came through the door and looked around at the tables, empty and occupied. Jack Peavine waved him over.

Jerry Dye took it as good a time as any to shuffle off and "get back to her." He stubbed out his cigarette and rose and threw a ten-dollar bill down and left, taking his chopped organ with him.

Clifford sat at the opposite head of the table, though situated more squarely, than Jerry had. His hair was still full and mostly red except where he'd grayed at the temples. Ike had always remembered him in his OHP uniform, with schooner wagons on the sleeves. Now though, Clifford wore starched jeans, clean boots, and a faded checkered cotton button-up shirt. Lola brought him a cup of coffee without having come to take the order from him.

"Young man—you still hot-roddin' around?" Clifford nodded toward Ike with a twinkle in his eye.

One of the last times Ike had seen Clifford Blow he was in the passenger seat of his buddy J.C.'s Z71, JC driving, a suitcase of beer behind the bench seat under a blanket.

"Dangerous comin' acrost the bridge that quick," Clifford had said, shining his light first at JC, then at Ike, holding it on Ike once he recognized Abe Dyson's boy from the coffee shop. "You oughtta know better, Dyson," he'd said.

Ike caught himself dazed at the memory and staring

at Clifford Blow whose eyes appeared to want an answer to the question. A wave of euphoria hit Ike. He tried to be cool. "Oh no—too old for that shit."

Old Clifford was satisfied and thumped Sweet'n'Low into his black coffee.

"You're daddy know you're out runnin' the highway?" Clifford had asked Ike that night across J.C., still holding the light on the Dyson boy.

"Oh—" Ike had paused. His dad didn't know he was out, but then, his daddy never really knew when he was out unless Ike was staying with his daddy, which he hadn't been then. He and J.C. had run over to Oklahoma that night to score weed off a buddy's cousin that went to school in Madill. Ike's mom and stepdad just thought he was staying at a buddy's house and J.C. had told his folks the same. They were ultimately planning to head back to their friend Trent's house in Whitesboro. Trent's mom worked all night and his dad lived in a trailer out at the lake, so the boys could party at Trent's house. But Ike saw an opportunity and lied, "Yea—I'm actually headed there now. He's takin' us huntin' in the mornin'." Ike was hoping Clifford would give him a break for speeding and not try to nose around the truck too much.

Clifford was correctly certain Abe hadn't hunted much in awhile, but he also knew he wasn't writing Abe Dyson's boy a ticket. Abe had bailed out too many troopers with that wrecker. Clifford told Ike and J.C. to slow down and good luck huntin'.

Abe broke the flashback, "Last time you seen this one he was just drivin'." Abe said it to Clifford while nodding at Ike.

Clifford was thinking the same as Ike: "Comin' too fast across the Willis Bridge I recall."

"I wasn't drivin' now," Ike shot back playfully and in his defense. Though, of course, there were times when he was the one driving and got out of the ticket on account of his daddy being the tow truck driver for local police, sheriff, and highway patrol and knowing practically everyone otherwise on account of Abe Dyson growing up around Oakland and Madill since high school and repairing near everyone's cars the last however many years.

"Well, ya'll hear about that 'ol Mexican boy was shot over at Oakland?" Clifford asked the table, shifting from his teasing of Abe's son. He may have been retired, but he still made all matter of local incident his business.

"Oh yea," Jack Peavine said as if the conversation had already passed through the diner that day, which it had.

Jack and Clifford looked to Abe. He hadn't heard with all he'd been distracted by, even though of the bunch at the table he was the only one actually lived in Oakland. "Nah—I ain't heard. He survive?" Abe figured he'd had too much commotion around his own lot to have paid much attention to much else, even a few blocks away.

"They don't know—can't find his ass." Clifford tilted his head to the side as he said this as if he felt it was shame and he raised the coffee that'd been brought to him and sipped.

"Really? What was it over?" Abe was interested.

"Lover's quarrel is the word, two fellas fightin' over a little Mexican girl," Jack Peavine said with a grin. "Illegals—both of 'em," he added with no malice.

"Two .44 slugs in the chest and they ain't got a body—either a tough Mexican headed south or he's at the bottom of Lake Texoma," theorized Clifford.

"And I suppose local law ain't gonna spend much resources chasin' after an illegal," Ike chimed in. The other men at the table took a bit of a start to Ike's two cents but recovered quickly enough this wasn't noted.

"Hell no," Clifford agreed and confirmed.

Just then Lee Pitchman came in. Ike hadn't seen him in years, but he smiled when he saw him. Lee had always been around his dad's shop. Had always been one of his dad's buds. In this moment of reunion, after all these years, Ike realizes Lee Pitchman was really like an uncle to him. His favorite uncle now that he thought on it.

Lee was unchanged except looking older. He wore his pocketed black t-shirt, his stained work jeans, a pair of workboots with the jeans tucked in, and a ratty faded black cowboy hat pushed back on his head.

His behavior was apparently unchanged too. He was here for his sweet tea for his blackened and smudged Styrofoam cup. Lee didn't care for the food at the diner choosing instead something fried from the Oakland Grocery's warm deli gas station fare for meals. However, he liked the sweet tea at the diner and would bring in the greasy foam cup he picked up and filled at the Oakland Grocery every morning and continued to refill at the gas station or diner throughout the day, whichever was nearest.

"Well speakin' of illegal," Jack Peavine said warmly, holding court at the diner table welcoming Lee.

"You know it," Lee shot back and grinned as he made his way over. "You're losing some weight," he said as he sat next to Ike. He said it as if it hadn't been years since they'd seen each other.

"Yea, left it all over the country, Lee," Ike said, not minding Lee pointing it out though it'd embarrassed him a bit when Abe had. Ike grinned.

Lee'd been called lots of names over the years. His

ex-wife probably developed most of them. "Wild Child" was always the one that stuck, though a few called him by "Snuff" regularly because he'd once fixed a leaky radiator cap with a can of dip. Ike always called him "Lee," and in the diner now again realizes this is a way he'd treated him as an uncle, calling him by first name when everyone else called him something else.

Lee Pitchman, as most know the story, come by his most common name in an Amarillo steakhouse.

Abe and Lee'd been tandem driving, delivering a load of trailer chassis they'd welded with CW when both worked there right out of high school. They'd made their delivery in Amarillo and had the company dollar on the generosity of Big Jim Canaan and Old Man Wheeler to grab a motel room for the night.

Lee offered to pick up dinner after they'd dropped their load. To Abe's surprise, Lee suggested an expensive steakhouse. Abe objected at such expense, but Lee insisted.

Well, the menu made Abe object again. Lee'd spend nearly all he made in pay on the trip just for steaks. They could grill cheap grocery steaks on the communal grill at the motel for a fraction of all that.

Lee wouldn't budge. They'd had a good trip, were making good money for being just out of school. This was a celebration.

Abe relented and ordered a small steak when the waiter came. Lee got a big one. Abe had to admit the steak was good though it tasted of guilt. Lee ate his with relish. Curiously, after he finished, he asked the waiter for another one, but much rarer.

This was brought.

Abe didn't ask at this point and let Lee play out whatever wild hair he had. Though he didn't expect what come.

Before Abe realized what was happening, Lee snatched the second steak from the plate in the waiter's hands and jumped down on the floor with it. He crawled under the table, dropped the steak, lunged toward it on all fours, began snarling and growling and barking and howling like a wild dog and then bit the steak off the floor. He began eating the bloody steak like a hungry animal.

The wait staff and customers panicked and buzzed uncomfortably. Abe dropped his cigarette when he jumped back from the table.

Lee continued on and the manager ran out from the kitchen.

"Get this Wild Child out of here!" he shouted more in exasperation than command when he finally surmised where and what the commotion radiated from.

Abe helped the waiter drag Lee to the parking lot while Lee continued to snarl rabidly, all the while holding the second half-chewed steak in his teeth.

As soon as they'd cleared the door to the parking lot by a few yards the waiter dumped his half of Lee and ran back inside. No bill was ever given or paid. Abe and Lee scooted before the cops come, if they were called.

As Abe and Lee shared the story over the years, "Wild Child" stuck, everyone who already knew Lee or would meet him finding it appropriate.

"We best get going," Abe said suddenly. Lee coming

in and being really the only other one besides Sara to see some of what had gone on made the thoughts of the Sledges and Canaan and the highway weigh heavier on him. Though he didn't know what was to come next, something was coming and he needed to figure a way to deal with it.

"Runnin' off already?" Clifford asked with his usual smirk though Ike could swear he heard something like concern in the old trooper's tone.

"Gotta get to it," Abe offered as Ike stood with him. Abe placed cash on the table to cover he and Ike.

"I'll be by after while or tomorrow mornin'," Wild Child called after. The announcement wasn't necessary, but it was something to say to his friend as Abe and Ike were on their way out.

"Yea," Abe called back in reply.

Ike gave a casual wave.

As they went out the door of the diner Ike turned back and saw Clifford lean in as if to ask Wild Child a question. Jack Peavine was still smiling warmly.

They'd already made the turn on 70 to head back to the Dyson lot when Abe realized Ike'd asked about the post office. It was Saturday which meant the post office had been closed since ten a.m., a fact neither Abe nor Ike had hit on when Ike mentioned it earlier. "I know you mentioned the post office earlier, but it won't be open again 'til Monday."

"Yea, I figured," Ike replied, though he didn't look very concerned about it and in fact hadn't thought about it since he'd asked. Now he was thinking about Lee Pitchman and Jack Peavine and Jerry Dye and Clifford Blow and what kind of lives they might lead. They were all single. Jack Peavine had been married six or seven times—two or three times to the same woman. Once only for a night. Jerry Dye was more pathetic. He and his partially severed organ were never married. Clifford had been married years and years before his wife died of cancer. The story always was Lee was still married to his wife because he wouldn't give her a divorce, but they hadn't lived together really since Ike could remember knowing Lee. Apparently the final straw occurred one night before Ike come along when Lee'd parked a one-ton International diesel Ford in front of the trailerhouse door where he and his bride lived so as to keep his bride trapped inside while he went out and partied. Divorced or not, she was referred to as the "ex-wife."

Ike knew all of this of these men, these characters, and wondered how he knew all of this.

When they pulled on to the lot a few minutes later, King was barking like mad up by the house, something he normally didn't do recognizing the sound of Abe's Bronco. When they reached the carport from the shop where Abe habitually parked, the storm door was swung open and the backdoor ajar.

Abe looked around his lot to account for any visitor. The customer cars radiated out from the shop. The impound gate was closed, and the chain appeared to be wrapped and padlocked still. The Sledge truck and other impounds were still there. The shop bay doors were all down and the office door on the west wall of the building remained shut. The rusting cars waiting for Abe to file storage and haul to scrap were still sitting, rusting. There didn't appear to be a visitor vehicle on the lot. Abe looked back to the open door of his house.

"The hell happened here?" Ike said, catching up after his own survey of the property. King was still barking but not as wildly and once he realized his master was on the carport he wormed his way out through the partially opened door.

Abe figured whoever'd been here wasn't still or King wouldn't come out that way. He'd still be barking at the intruder. Abe felt okay going in but made sure to lead his son.

Inside, the house was fairly trashed. Cabinet and hutch doors were open, shit spilled on the floor. Drawers were left dangling with their contents strewn.

"I need to check something in the shop," Abe said quickly and headed back out towards the shop on the back of the lot without answering his son's question.

Ike stood and rolled a cigarette and lit it and smoked. Then he began to sort of pick things up with his free hand, assembling and piling things on the round table in the dining area off the back of the living room and side of the kitchen galley.

He did so with little order or concern for the contents initially, though certain items began to catch his eye. He found the old photos he'd been shown as a kid of his dad riding bulls at the Madill and Kingston and Ardmore rodeos. Abe would have been in his early or mid-twenties in these. He read snippets of a recent newspaper clipping Sara had saved about the summer's previous drought. It told of and showed a couple of small photos of how bits of Woodville, OK, a town intentionally abandoned and flooded to build the lake, had started to show from the drastically low tides of Lake Texoma. Tombstones, windows, and old clapboards were all stuck in red mud normally covered by lake water.

A photograph he found of his young grandfather, Shorty, sitting on the hood of an old Chevy with his older brother, JL, made Ike think back. His grandfather was jolly. As a kid, Ike'd always liked when his grandpa was around, though it wasn't much since he'd lived in northwestern Oklahoma most all of Ike's life. As far as Ike remembered it, his grandpa had moved up there right before or after Ike'd been born.

Ike thought about freshman year of high school. Inhumation is another word for funeral but it oughtta be another word for freshman year.

The dance Ike is at has turned into the sepulture he should of gone to. The mum Ike's date wears says *Homecoming apostrophe 94* on its ribbons but all Ike can see when he sees it is his grandfather's obit and the sad look on his dad's mug when Ike said he wasn't going to the funeral. He had a date.

Unbeknownst to Ike the day Ike's dad showed up after school with the bad news Ike's date wished evil on Ike with her friends in the girls locker room because Ike let slip to some buddies in the boys locker room he'd messed around with her on the school bus on the field trip and it got around school. Ike Dyson is already paying for the sins of his youth with the blood of his family.

The cafetorium becomes a crematorium as Ike tries to choke down powdery punch and sweats through his shirt. The lights are out. His date has abandoned him—sorry to herself she'd wished him bad when she'd heard about his grandpa but still wanting him hanged for being an ornery boy.

As Ike hangs alone he hears exequies and obsequies of family over the slow dance choice.

Ike Dyson feels all the worse being old enough to see he is the cause of his own funeration this night. He looks around in a sweaty and suffocated haze wondering who here will give him last rites.

Ike feels depressed and puts the photograph on the table carefully and continues the chore at hand.

Out back Abe unlocked the big industrial knob of the shop's thick steel office door. He glanced around enough to see nothing was out of place from last he'd seen it, and it appeared so. He kept the shop and impound locked well for the sake of customers' property and to guard against impound thieving, though had for years neglected to lock his own house doors. He unlocked the fire box in the corner of the office under the desk and found the brown accordion folder where he'd shoved all the briefcase's contents safe.

He glanced at the briefcase on top of his desk. Once again he felt the urge to get rid of it. Ike said something earlier that day on the way to the Bronco to go to the diner about visiting a high school buddy some time that night. Abe could burn or dump the case or something then. Now he wondered how he'd play this with his son, just returned home in the middle of this mess.

He closed and locked the fire box. He carefully remembered to lock the shop door on the way out. He walked around to impound, unlocked the padlock on the gate, and walked over to the truck. The tailgate and camper lid were still open, though it appeared more of the dog food might have been sloshed around from the cardboard box where Abe'd found the briefcase buried. As he walked back on the worn path from the shop's office door to the house's back door inside the open carport, he decided not to tell Ike anything about it yet, to let him run off and have fun with whoever before worrying him any with it, if at all.

He wondered if anyone on the surrounding block

saw anything but decided it wasn't worth asking. Despite the mess inside the house, this wouldn't have really been a loud crime. Abe figured folks were so used to seeing various vehicles on his lot come and go by his trade that it would be impossible for them to see if a suspicious vehicle was on the lot.

"They get into the shop too?" Ike asked still fairly casual about everything, still picking items up here and there and placing them in a heap on the table. Occasionally he thought to close the nearest drawer or cabinet door and things were starting to look somewhat picked up.

"Naw. That thing stays plenty locked," Abe replied acknowledging in tone his habit of not locking the house.

"You think it was meth heads or pill scroungers?" Ike's question offered exactly the lie Abe had thought to tell. Abe felt a great deal of relief.

"Probably so, the way it's just ransacked but nothin' really gone. Ya know? Can't think who'd have kids around here to do something like this if they knew me. There are a few new folks've moved in though. Mostly Mexican workers in trailers." Abe realized he was probably offering too much and left it at that.

"Sorry, Dad," Ike offered having seemed to stop cleaning. "I'm going to go take a shower, then I'll finish cleaning up in here before I take off after while."

"No no, thanks for this. Just clean yourself up and go have fun with your buddy." Abe meant it.

Ike wondered why the shelf had fallen in the bathroom when he undressed. As he showered he noted the small window above the shower wall had a small hole and crack. He surmised correctly a bullet must have come through the window. He didn't know if that was connected to the shelf down or not, if that was part of today's ransacking or not.

The shower felt good. Ike had been on the road and it was refreshing to wash it off. He smiled at the big bar of Lava soap in the shower, all he could remember his dad using, all that was strong enough to get all that oil and grime off his dad's big mechanic's hands.

Ike put on a fresh set of underwear and a fresh black t-shirt, and then pulled on the same jeans he'd been wearing. He put his grandpa's boots on again and took off for the evening.

After Ike'd left, the house was quiet. Abe noted Ike'd managed to get quite a bit picked up. Nothing was in its place but the doors and drawers were mostly closed and the pile of junk on the table was more orderly than all the junk being flung everywhere.

Abe watched TV for an hour or so before debating cleaning up more or trying to take another quick nap in his recliner, the only way he'd managed any sleep the last couple days.

The phone rang.

Abe answered without letting it ring many times though he didn't make a hurry of it. King sat up on the floor of the living room looking cross until the ringing stopped. He hated the noise and it wasn't helped by the fact that Abe had a loudener on it to make sure the phone woke him in case of a wrecker call in the middle of the night, which was when most impounds or bad wrecks seemed to happen. King laid back down once Abe answered.

"'Lo," Abe answered in the way he answered every phone call.

"Abe—hey—we made it." Sara was calling from New Mexico to check in.

Abe looked at the time—it was coming up on six. Abe tried to remember if Sara was an hour or two behind now. "You're an hour behind there right?" he asked correctly.

"Yea—coming up on five here." Sara was almost always cheery in tone. Abe found it refreshing.

"How was the drive?"

"Made it in about twelve hours—like you said."

Abe may have lived most of his life on his lot, but a couple years driving trailers across the south and southwest after high school, tandem driving with Wild Child mostly, had made him an expert at road travel and time. Made him aware of where some things were in this part of the country.

"No car problems?" It was an obligatory question not only because he was her husband but because Abe's occupational hazard was folks' car problems, especially before and after long trips. Abe knew now of course that if there had been any for Sara and her sister Sara would've already mentioned it. He was making conversation to avoid Sara asking after the Sledges or the truck impound.

"No," Sara confirmed, then asked, "Anything else with the Sledges and that truck?"

Abe didn't want to lie to his wife. He certainly didn't need to shield her from the hardscrabble ways of folks around these parts. She knew the country well and grew up a little rough herself before her and Abe were hitched. He hadn't thought to shield her from anything in seventeen years of marriage. But he certainly didn't want her to worry over a little ransacking while she was at a family wedding, and though his anxieties about it were growing, the Sledges hadn't done anything drastic or harmful yet.

"Nah—told you they were just drunk and jackin' off. Sober, that truck ain't worth much to 'em I'm sure."

Abe thought again of throwing off the case somewhere. He thought he might take a drive and drop it in the lake.

"Good. Had a terrible feeling something awful was coming. Maybe it's just my blood pressure." Sara was half Choctaw and generally trusted her feeling and premonition, though high blood pressure in the past few years got in the way of premonitions.

"Your sister do okay with the trip?" Abe again sought to distract from such talk.

"Oh yea. In fact, she's waiting to use the phone to call her kids. I should probably let you go. Just wanted to let you know we made it." Sara still had the cheer and Abe was glad she'd called now. It calmed him he realized.

"Well say 'hey' to your family for me."

"Will do. Love you."

"Love you too." Abe let Sara hang up first, then hung the phone back on the wall and finished getting the mess off the floor.

With no better system in mind, Abe continued with Ike's method, heaping stuff on the table, regardless of where it would eventually need to return.

Something hit on Abe and he walked to the back bedroom, Ike's old room. Sara had Abe move the gun cabinet in there from the living room shortly after she moved in.

The thick metal cabinet had clearly held and it's lock, though it may have looked scratched and picked at, obviously had as well. Abe pulled the set of keys from his pocket, located the cabinet's only copy, and unlocked it.

He cared little for the majority of the guns beyond their utility but wanted to make sure his grandma's Sears & Roebuck double-barrel rabbit-ear 1914 shotgun and his dad's war sabers were safe.

Shorty Dyson had won several battle stars. He'd served with the Sea Bees in the Pacific. He was mechanic by assignment, keeping landing craft in proper working order, often operating landing craft himself. Once on an island though, he was a fighter too.

He'd liberated the military sabers from two dead Japanese soldiers after one of the fights was over. One of the sabers was lifted from a private, the other, from an officer. Shorty'd sent them back home in a big crate packed with cheap base souvenirs. They were waiting for him when he returned home from the war. He'd given them to Abe before moving back to the family farm in Dewey County, hours north.

The shotgun and sabers were still in place. Abe closed the cabinet and locked it again, having touched nothing.

He returned to the living room. He gave King a scratch and resumed picking up the odds and ends of his storage units and countertops and side tables and such.

With nothing broken or shot up or attempted to be shot up, Abe figured this was on direct order from Shane, not a drunken whim like the previous night seemed to be. Shane'd probably told whoever he sent, if it wasn't Shane himself, to look for the case or its documents or the ledger book. Not to mess with nothing else.

Whoever had been here had rifled through near everything on the surface and openable, took nothing as far as Abe could tell, and intended no damage otherwise.

He thought again of asking a neighbor or two if they'd seen anything. He could be specific and ask after an orange GMC pickup or Scout or another Sledge vehicle, but Abe thought it was better to let it lie. He sat down again and stretched back in the recliner above King .

Abe lit a cigarette and began flipping through channels again.

He paid for expensive dish but he enjoyed a multitude of western and classic movie and history and military channels that way. He flipped dutifully through these but didn't pay much attention as he did so. He thought about his son being back. About his wife being gone. About taking a drive to the lake and dumping the Canaan briefcase. Maybe its contents too. He settled on Turner Classic Movies because they were showing *The Petrified Forest* which he'd seen a hundred times and could follow easy without really following.

He snubbed his cigarette in the ashtray on the side table.

He was asleep within minutes.

He dreamed of the time Ike was staying part of the summer with him and they went on a wrecker run at night together. There was a meth lab that'd been busted by the lake and Abe and Ike had rolled into a lot of action, gunfire and arrests still happening, just to impound the vehicle.

SATURDAY NIGHT

It took Abe a minute to get his senses when he awoke. King was already at the back door and Abe let him out, followed and monitored his urination, and promptly brought the dog back in so he could take a piss himself.

After relieving himself, Abe went to the kitchen and poured the last of the iced tea Sara had made before she left and drank it down with few gulps. The cold jangled his nose and almost overwhelmed his throat after a day of coffee and cigarettes.

Abe ambled around, changed his shirt, left King inside, and went back toward the shop to get the empty suitcase.

Abe thought about the dream of the memory he'd had as he drove out to the lake. He'd woke in the dusk, but now the sun had gone down. It'd taken him longer than it normally would to get dressed and moving around.

He drove past all the places he and Ike would have run past in the tow truck that night, more than fifteen years ago as best as Abe could think, young as Ike was at the time.

The diesel and coffee created a pleasant aroma for Abe Dyson, who was still picking crud from the corner of his eyes when he stepped out into the Oklahoma night in the Love's parking lot. Abe was always pleased when this scent hit him, although he never thought about that consciously.

The boy bounded out of the passenger door and went inside with a crumpled $5 bill from Abe. It was a routine by this point in the summer. Abe filled her up, Ike went and bought a couple of cokes.

Midnight runs had long ago lost their excitement for Abe who'd been driving the tow truck for a couple of years now. It had more than doubled the income of his shop. He didn't mind it—just wasn't excited by it like the boy anymore. The boy had made a few runs with him already that summer, and several the last. This summer he was staying with Abe practically the whole vacation. The boy was even proving useful help on the tow jobs and wreck clean-up, now that he'd had some practice and was around it routinely a couple years in a row.

"I got you Pepsi because there wasn't any bottles of Coke." The boy had apparently elected to buy himself a Chocolate Soldier.

"That's fine," Abe assured even though he knew he

wouldn't be drinking it. The boy never noticed that Abe rarely drank the soda the boy was sent to retrieve. It was too sweet for Abe these days. "We're good to go. Load up."

Marshall County is the smallest county in Oklahoma. Still, the OHP had told Abe that this one was all the way out toward the lake near Buncombe Creek. Abe figured they had another fifteen minutes or so to go once he opened it up on 377, south of town.

"What we got? A wreck?"

Abe was surprised the boy hadn't asked already once he had.

"No, meth cookers. Got a lab out at Buncombe." Abe was trying to figure out how much he might need to explain on that and was relieved when the boy had no follow-up questions.

For his part, the boy was imagining a real laboratory, same as where they make medicine, just one that made meth, which the boy had only a vague notion of.

They were half-way to the lake when dispatch barked at Abe on the CB mounted to the roof of the Ford diesel's cab: "Dyson, what's your twenty?"

Abe was annoyed. This is why OHP was his least favorite. The Madill Police were the best because they were never in a hurry. It was always something around town. Sheriff's usually only call on abandoned stuff, so there's no one waiting on the tow truck at all. Oklahoma Highway Patrol was always in a damned hurry—wrecks and stranded motorists and such.

"OHP-this is Abe-about seven miles away. Had to fuel."

"Oh that's fine." That caught Abe off-guard. Dispatch was relieved he wasn't closer. The answer came before Abe could ask any question: "In fact, take your time. We still got some sortin' to do out here." This was Clifford, the veteran trooper. He'd come in on the transmission to fill Abe in out of courtesy.

So Abe was relieved again. Dispatch had sent him a little early, so, rightly or not, there wouldn't be any pissed off troopers waiting. He figured.

"What are they sortin'?" The boy had been quiet, daydreaming, to the point that Abe had almost forgotten his presence. He wondered what the boy would tell his mother. He hoped the boy told his mother as little as possible. He couldn't do much else other than leave the boy at night, or bring him with, he figured.

"Oh, probably got three or four boys in one vehicle—need another patrol car to haul 'em away or something." It was a perfectly rational thought for Abe to have, even though that wouldn't turn out to be the problem. Abe was relieved in knowing though that it was a simple drug case impound, not a wreck or anything to sort out. Straight impound was always the easiest run to make. Just back up to the vehicle and take it. No clean ups or damaged cars that won't roll straight or people bleeding and crying and dying. The boy liked wrecks best. He got to sweep the highway, direct traffic, crawl under rolled-over trucks to attach J-hooks and wench cables and chains. Abe didn't need much help with plain old impounds.

"Where's the lab at?" The boy was still picturing a clinical facility.

"Probably just some old trailer off the road."

The boy was disappointed but didn't respond. He was still trying to picture everything. He would see soon, though the trip was seeming to take much longer for the boy than for Abe.

Abe slowed the wrecker and threw on the left turn signal though there were absolutely no other cars to signal to on 377 this late at night. The road in front and behind pulsed yellow and red in the darkness.

"We close?" the boy wanted to know.

"Think so." This would have been Abe's reply no matter the case, but he meant it this time.

They were on Shay Cut-off Road now. Abe used to come out here in high school for lake and pasture parties. This was one of the rural routes they took on Saturday nights to Henderson's old place. They could drink beer and smoke cigarettes on the back pasture there without anyone to see or get them in trouble. He'd drive the Corvair out here.

Abe was thinking about his old Corvair—how he used to drive nintey miles an hour down this gravel. The Corvair had the rear-mounted engine, like a VW Bug, so the front-end would dance all over the gravel at high speeds, unless they had a few cases of beer thrown up front to weigh it down. Which they often did.

"I ever tell you I had a '66 Corvair?" Abe had, but he'd mentioned lots of cars to the boy. He couldn't keep track.

"Yea." The boy wasn't totally sure, because he couldn't keep track either, but it seemed like a safe bet to just answer in the affirmative. The boy was distracted because the road was starting to look familiar to him too. He was starting to realize he wasn't going to see anything new or exciting. There weren't any clinics or labs out here. There couldn't be some big TV police style raid going on.

Abe, already expecting the familiarity of the land, was now questioning his sense of direction and time. He felt they should have seen the turn for Enos Road which run to the thinly populated trailer park they were headed to, as OHP described. Abe visualized it from his youth. In his middle-age now though, he didn't necessarily always trust the memory of his youth. He decided to hold out for another quarter mile before trying to turn the big Ford wrecker around on the narrow gravel road. Lo and behold he hadn't missed Enos and he took it.

"How far…" The boy didn't finish his question, nor did he need to. There were red and blue and light-colored lights dancing all over the sticky junipers.

"Roll up your window," Abe said unnecessarily as the boy was already doing so instinctually.

The limestone gravel crunched and turned over stone by stone as the one-ton wrecker rolled to a stop in the middle of a long driveway, about a half-mile down Enos. Then Abe and the boy heard noises.

Poppoppitypop. Pop. Poppitypop. Staccato revolver and automatic handgun fire volleyed back and forth.

There were bright flashes in the pitch black to the right of the trailerhouse ahead. There was gunfire returned out the open side door under the yellow bug light on the right end of the trailer. The boy immediately swung a gawking face at Abe.

Abe tried to stay calm so the boy wouldn't get too excited: "Looks like they called us too soon. They haven't gotten custody, let alone hauled these guys away yet." Abe threw the wrecker in reverse and rolled backwards fifty yards or so, just to make sure they were clear of ricochet.

The two could still see into the clearing where the trailer was stationed. There was more gunfire. Then the troopers moved in. Eight or nine Oklahoma Highway Patrolmen overwhelmed the front door. It was only ninety seconds or so before they emerged with two guys zip tied at the hands. As they came out the front, a figure bailed out the side door, over the porch railing, and disappeared into the briar and brush that threatened to close in on the yard.

The two that were tied, Abe and the boy noticed, had little round welts on their shirtless chests. The one with longer hair had one right over his heart. The other one was more in the center of the torso and down. They were welts from the non-lethal beanbag guns troopers carried. Abe knew this, but the boy was left to wonder why they had two such similar scars.

"Go after the runner!" Abe heard one of the troopers yell. By now Abe was standing beside the cab of the truck, where he'd moved automatically in a way, out of some curiosity or drive to be part of the action. He'd made the boy stay in the cab.

"Reach me that revolver from the glove box," he said through the driver's window, which he'd left down.

The boy reached for the glove box, and with very little expression, pulled the .45 long-snout revolver Abe carried in the wrecker, just in case. It was the gun and clip-on holster and all. He passed it to his dad through the driver's window. Abe slipped the clip of the holster into his front pocket and let the revolver hang there. It made his legs feel shorter.

"Who went out the side door?" the boy asked through the window.

Abe just shrugged at him. The troopers were spreading out behind the trailer, about to search through the brush. The two apprehended were already in the back of a car.

As Abe watched after the troopers, wondering how long it was going to be before he and the boy could get the car out of the driveway, he felt a presence. A minute and a half or two minutes maybe had passed.

Abe Dyson turned to see a rough, shirtless, twenty-something boy with darker skin standing next to him. He recognized him as Danny Tulip Jr. Abe sold his and Agatha's trailerhouse to Danny Tulip Sr. and the Tulip family once Abe'd built the house on the lot. From what Abe'd known, Danny Tulip had moved the trailer across the lake to the Texas side and the shabby lake community of Sherwood Shores, mostly trailers and small clapboard houses.

"What's going on here?" Danny Jr. asked Abe casually as he could though could not hide a quiver in his voice.

"Looks like they're having trouble getting everyone," Abe said to him, knowing he was the runner.

"Well...shit," the shirtless Danny Tulip Jr. said after another twenty seconds or so, "Guess I better just make it easy."

"Guess so." Abe didn't know why he encouraged him to do so other than it seemed that was what Danny Jr. wanted to do anyway.

Danny Jr. walked down the drive. As he approached the clearing and the trooper waiting by the car, he threw his hands up in the air, but not suddenly or in a panic, more in the casual grace of a scolded dog.

Abe was too far away to hear anything that was said, but as the dark skinned runner had his hands in the air, the nearest trooper grabbed for the mace on his belt and blasted Danny Tulip Jr. in the eyes.

Danny Jr. fell down screaming and rolling in the grass. The trooper decided to not make it easy after all.

Abe glanced from the side of his eye so as not to add to the excitement into the cab of the wrecker at the boy who was wide-eyed.

Abe spoke up so the boy could hear him on the passenger side of the cab through the driverside window: "Don't tell your mother about this." He didn't bark this, but half-smiled as he said it.

But the boy was too worked up to regard it and had to ask, "Why'd they pepper-spray that guy...he was turnin' hisself in wasn't he?"

"Don't know." This seemed like as good an explanation as any. "Don't worry, he'll be okay soon. It's not permanent." This was true, which Abe knew, and the boy would have to trust.

Abe handed the pistol, holster and all, back to his son, now that everything was settled and everyone was in cuffs and in the backseats of cars. Clifford, older and less excitable than the younger troopers he led, dunked a red bandana he pulled from his pocket into a beer cooler on the porch of the trailer to wet it and gave Danny Tulip Jr. some relief by placing it over his face in the back seat. Ike put the gun back into the glovebox.

"Anyway, don't tell your mother," Abe offered again.

"I won't," the boy accepted.

Once the cruisers had backed out of the driveway onto the gravel road, Abe popped the emergency brake, eased in the clutch, and rolled the heavy wrecker down the driveway, toward the clearing with the trailer and the car.

It took Abe and the boy four or five minutes to hoist up the Mercury Sable they'd been called to impound. It was front wheel drive, so all that was needed was the pneumatic lift under the front wheels, and the back would roll, just like a trailer. The boy helped by extending the lift arms and locking them into place once they were securely under the front wheels, though this would have only taken a minute or two longer if Abe had had to do it by himself, as he usually did. While Abe backed and turned the Ford and its Mercury tow around, the boy stared at the bullet holes in the aluminum siding of the trailerhouse. They were smaller than he had imagined they should be.

"That one with the shaved head and darker skin?" It was a question. Abe was asking his son about the boy that had been pepper sprayed and dunked. They were about three miles back up 377 toward Madill.

The boy led him on, even though he didn't get as good a look to describe the guy as Abe had: "Yea?"

"That's Danny Tulip's boy." Abe Dyson said this as if the boy would know him though he wasn't sure.

The boy reacted as if this was so because he did know. "Oh yea?" Ike went to school with Benny Tulip, Danny Tulip Jr.'s younger brother. Ike had been pushed off a fence rail at school by Benny just a couple years prior and had to spend a painful afternoon in the emergency room with his uncertain stepdad to make sure he wasn't gonna wind up retarded from the wound on his head. It wound up a mild concussion.

"Yea—always heard he was runnin' with a rough crowd," Abe offered.

"Too bad," said the boy shaking his head.

It was like they were having a real conversation. They continued the drive home in the dark.

Abe and Ike didn't talk much in the times between Ike's visits.

Abe never really got a good feel for what Ike's home-life with his mother and stepdad was. Abe knew he felt uncomfortable going there to pick Ike up for his son's summer and holiday visits, but then, he and Agatha never really got along anyway and his uncomfortable-ness just seemed a natural byproduct of that.

Ike must not of told his mom about the Buncombe Creek shootout because Abe knew he'd of caught hell if she knew about that one.

Must have been two or three summers before the night at Buncombe that Abe had let Ike stay up all night with him, watching a John Wayne marathon. He caught an earful from Agatha for that. Same as getting him the pellet air revolver when Ike was nine, or the dirt bike summer. Agatha let Abe hear about those too. Seemed strange to Abe that Ike always seemed to have so much fun around him, but after his momma'd get mad about it, Ike wouldn't be as interested in the gun or the motorcycle anymore the next summer. Or maybe it just seemed that way to Abe.

These thoughts pinged about in his head as he rattled down the dark highway then were pushed out as he came to a new detour. Must have come up that day or the day before because Abe knew he'd just run by here a few days ago. He slowed the Bronco and gradually stopped at the barricade suggesting he turn right, down Old Willis Road off 377. This would mean taking Old Willis around a bend of trees, past some gravel drives that provided access to some rural farm roads and private properties, then on back around to 377 a little nearer to the lake on the other side of whatever the construction was.

But Abe saw nothing that looked like road construction, saw no big equipment or piles of rock from a day of road building. He figured the barricades were up in anticipation of work to be done the next day and so just skirted around the barricade and stayed on the highway slowing down again only to make sure he cleared the barricade a mile or so down the road attempting to sway northbound traffic to the same Old Willis Road detour. He ran into no other cars. Clear of the phantom construction zone he was only a few minutes north of the bridge. With the window down Abe could smell the muddy lake in the air.

The lake was muddy because it was fed by a muddy river, the Red River. To save the area from river flood waters and produce electricity, at some point at the end of the 1930s the Red River was dammed at the Denison spillway and a lake was planned by the Army Corps of Engineers. The name that made most sense was what locals had already begun to call their borderland-- *Texoma*.

The clearing and digging began six or seven years later, amid World War II.

The shovel diggers and timber cutters were Nazis--German Prisoners of War captured in North Africa and held in various camps in the area. The reason for this was that the Geneva Convention demanded POWs be held in climates similar to capture. Apparently Texoma's climate matched North Africa's well enough.

With American engineering and Nazi labor, Lake Texoma had been completed and filled in just five years from ground busting.

Now, where the Washita conflues with the Red River, stood a lake. A big one. Forty-six thousand hectacres. Big enough to drown cars and bodies and culpability. State troopers and game wardens could drag it, could find things, often did. But the muddy red lake waters took time to search--long enough to dissolve evidence and create distance and muddle investigations.

Abe needed the papers, needed the notes, needed the steel company man's books--but he didn't need the briefcase. It was too noteable, too traceable. He cut the Bronco's lights as he halted it near the northside of the Willis Bridge on the thin strip of Oklahoma highway shoulder available.

He sat and stared at the dark water a moment and then the bridge. He'd recalled many times the story of Clifford Blow taking out the bank robber on this same stretch of road. Clifford had been a young trooper then. He was old now.

Apparently, a few years after the bridge was completed here across the lake, a bank robber from Gainesville, Texas was making a run across the border in his big Pontiac with a good lead on Grayson County Texas sheriff's deputies. Clifford picked it up on his radio while he was prowling on a dirt road off the highway a few miles north of the lake and put his foot into the V8 Chevy patrol car.

As the robber's Pontiac crested the hill just south of the lake on Texas 377 Clifford was at the bottom of the hill between the Willis filling station and Last Call Saloon on the Oklahoma side, both tearing up road as fast as they could. The robber had less road to cover before the bridge and was nearly halfway across the lake and bridge before Clifford come within a half mile. The robber was three-quarters across when Clifford was still a quarter mile shy and slammed on his brakes and cut the big wheel left. The robber in the Pontiac slammed on his brakes but couldn't help skidding the last eighth mile, broadsiding the passenger side of Clifford's patrol car at high speed.

The impact bloodied the robber's face and knocked him out. Clifford broke his left collarbone and separated his shoulder when he slammed into the Chevy's steel driver's side door. Still, Clifford managed to crawl out of the steel spun wreckage with one arm and draw his gun down on the groggy robber while Texas troopers caught up and crossed over the bridge.

Abe thought about that story every time he crossed the lake here. He thought about it now as he crawled out of the Bronco with the empty briefcase and the smell of lake again overwhelmed and aroused him.

As he walked across the bridge towards its center he marveled at how the ride across wasn't bumpier with the potholes, swollen pothole fills, and cracks in the pavement. He stopped where he thought the middle might be and peered over the rusty railguard into the dark water. He'd known a lot of stories of folks throwing things off here. The truck and blown safe from the robbery of Canaan had been found underwater near here. Abe wondered how the Sledges managed to roll that truck over the bridgerail without doing damage. He thought too that there was probably more from the robbery that'd been cast off in the lake that either the water already eat up or just hadn't been found when the truck and safe were recovered. He'd heard tell that paintings and lots of valuable objects were taken in the robbery, or at least, not accounted for in the rubble of the fire of the big Canaan house. Abe thought the Sledges probably had to throw a lot of that stuff off. They couldn't of sold it local without whoever buying knowing who it would belong to. It was too small a world down here. And the Sledges wouldn't of known how to sell it off outside the local. Unless they were holding on to the paintings and other items like the briefcase, Abe thought those were probably getting wet and eroded at the bottom of the lake.

He reared his left arm back and hurled the briefcase

discus-style. He thought maybe a couple of seconds passed before the smack of the leather hitting the water echoed up.

He wheeled on his boot heels and stalked back to his Bronco--still ticking and cooling from the seventeen mile ride out to the bridge. Still, no one came to pass from either direction and Abe wheeled the Bronco around, shoulder to shoulder, and headed back north on 377 as unnoticed as he'd come.

He dashed around and through the constructions zone barricades when he come upon them again.

Two miles west of Madill, where 377 stops heading north and curves east toward town, Abe started to take the turn for the rural residential road that bypassed the western edge of Madill back to his shop. The road that would be widened to Business 70 according to the Canaan plan. The road that would take his property. At the last moment though he continued on the bend toward Madill and the diner. He thought he'd get some coffee.

Abe turned left at the split of 377 and 70, north toward the diner. He passed through Madill in the dark, brightened at intervals with the orange glow of street lamps and a couple of open liquor stores and gas stations. Francis, Burney, Tishomingo, Taliaferro, Lillie, and Overton Streets pass by before Abe slows and puts his blinker on just south of the Drew Street intersect where Hobo Joe's diner sits toward the north end of town, the less busy end.

"Abe—you're out late. Wrecker run?" Clifford was posted-up at a four-top in the otherwise empty diner. As the nightshift waitress, Krystal knew Clifford sat up most nights here after his wife had passed. This night Clifford knew full well Abe hadn't been on a wrecker run. He was retired now, but he still had a scanner and radio, still caught all the busts, the wrecks, the impounds.

"Just can't sleep," Abe replied, knowing Clifford Blow knew he hadn't been called out.

"Wouldn't have anything to do with them dumb ass Sledge boys shootin' up your place now?"

"I didn't call that in, Officer Blow," Abe said, teasing, taking no real offence. Everybody's business got around. Hell, three or four neighbors coulda heard or seen the whole thing plain. Lee'd maybe told Old Clifford about it earlier in the day when he'd come into the diner as Abe and Ike were leaving.

"Sheriff Blow if you wanna go that far," Clifford said, referencing his last and highest rank with a lot of sparkle in his old eyes.

"Yea—hotheads wanted their truck back and didn't wanna pay for it. Shots fired was mostly their notion of having fun and showing off."

"That's all it was, was it?"

"Yea."

"Heard you licked Randy pretty good for it."

"Only on account Andy scampered away—he deserved it as much or more."

"Hard to think they wouldn't know better—dim bulbs they are. Must be a special truck."

Krystal, the night waitress, brought Abe a coffee cup and filled it from the pot in her other hand. Abe lit a cigarette and Clifford did likewise once his cup was topped off. Clifford smoked unfiltered Pall Malls. The tips of his thumb, pointer, and middle finger on his right hand were stained with tar.

"Who knows with the Sledges?" Abe offered after a few pulls from the cigarette and a sip from the cup.

"Well between barrelin' in here at high noon yesterday afternoon and having it out with Shane and Allie in the parking lot, then Randy and Andy shootin' your place up—well, I figure you got your finger in their eye some ways." Clifford smirked and sipped his coffee.

"So whaddaya know, *Sheriff* Blow?"

"Know they took your dog, know they tried to break into impound which is why they shot up your place, and took a good ass-whoopin' in the process—all for a rusty eight-hundred-dollar truck ain't gonna be worth its impound fee after tomorrow. Dumb as some of them Sledges is, they ain't doin' all that lest they got something in that truck that can get 'em hurt or get 'em money. Drugs or worse. You bein' your daddy's son and knowin' what you know from growin' up around here means you know that too." Clifford knew Shorty from around town but they'd also worked together some since Shorty was a volunteer sheriff's deputy. "Miss your daddy," Clifford said, as he did at some point in coffee shop conversation to Abe two or three times a year since Shorty'd passed.

Abe held a drag of his cigarette, drank his coffee, then allowed the smoke to escape his nostrils. "You musta run into Wild Child," he said, ignoring the comment of his dad.

"Just earlier in here when he come in," Clifford confirmed.

"Anyone else?" Abe hadn't told Lee not to spread it around, but then, he hadn't weighed all the gravity of it or known what the Sledges were comin' for at the time.

"Just Jack Peavine. And he's your friend. So's Wild Child and it ain't like he's just blabbin'," Clifford said reading Abe's mood about it. "He was comin' to me as a trusted knower of law enforcement and retired concerned citizen.

Besides, I asked him about you given I heard of all the commotion with the Sledges." Clifford leaned forward, seizing the opportunity in the conversation, and added, in a more grave tone, "My concern here is whether you know well enough to leave it at knowin' what might be or you done inventoried that truck and knowin' for sure is what's got you up tonight talkin' to an old retired widower at the coffee shop."

"Goddamned Sledges," Abe said over his coffee off into space without much malice about it.

"Shit. What the hell you in Abraham Dyson and why do I think you just wisht it was drugs?"

"Ain't good. Same time—" Abe said and broke off to take a last drag from his cigarette before snubbing it out in the black plastic diner ashtray. After a beat, he continued, "Something maybe I could use though. Need to know anyway," Abe finished, trailing off a bit in his tone.

Clifford pressed on, continued to hold the bulk of it: "Funny thing keeps ringin' out to me about the Sledges."

"Yea?" Abe suddenly realizes Clifford always knew where this was going, just workin' his way to it from the moment Abe came in the coffee shop.

"Keeps comin' to me they's somehow involved in the robbery and fire out at Canaan's place last summer."

"Really?" Abe kept letting Clifford work for it.

"Yea—be pretty clever for that bunch."

"Then again, you're tellin' me about it. Couldn't a-been too smart about it," Abe said, then asked, "Canaan know?"

Clifford smiled. "He 'spects."

"He tried you for it yet?"

"He knows better. I wouldn't investigate on his dime. Frank says he keeps danglin' for a local officer to have a run at it. They all think he's an ass mainly, but, a course, in the right circumstances any of 'em might take a bribe if Canaan ever decided it was time to throw money at it."

Frank Blow had followed in Clifford's footsteps and become a well-respected red-headed trooper as well. Clifford's son thus kept Clifford well informed.

"Course," Abe agreed and drank more of his coffee.

"Then, if the Sledges still got something Little Jim Canaan wants, and he finds out you got it, boy--" Clifford said, letting it trail off there.

"Yea, 'specially if it's something he wouldn't want people knowin', or seein'," Abe interjected.

Clifford agreed with this: "Exactly. And you think the Sledges is trouble? No tellin' who or what Little Jim could get after you with the right motivation. My question becomes, what could possibly be your motivation to hangin' on to such a foul object, Abe Dyson? Or objects, I suppose."

For all Clifford knew, he didn't yet know what Abe had indeed found that the Sledges wanted and that Little Jim would want worse when he got back to town. Abe figured it was best then to let Clifford know. He was at the end of his rope anyway with trying to figure what to do on his own. He felt a sudden ping of guilt that he'd kept it from his son.

Abe recounted with the best detail he could what he'd found. The briefcase. The memo outlining a new highway vein off 70 that connected to the wrap around of 377 on the south end of town and the strategy for grabbing the land along its stretch to do so. The ledger that suggested a certain amount of overpay to just the right folks. The motivation for the city to benefit in business and traffic from the new thoroughfare. Everything.

"It'd take my lot," Abe said toward the end of his

account. "And I'm not even listed as a specific obstacle in all this eminent domain," he added.

"I take it you mean to fight it." Clifford didn't ask this, more said it to himself.

"I don't imagine I couldn't," Abe confirmed.

Clifford leaned back after returning his coffee cup to its saucer. He pulled another cigarette from the pack inside his shirt pocket. He lit it and inhaled and flicked its ash into the ashtray very deliberately, considering the situation. Finally, he spoke up.

"I had to run for sheriff a few times. Well, I wanted to be sheriff and that's part of it anyway." Clifford looked to Abe for some sense of confirmation at this.

"Sure," Abe said.

"Well, I learned something about dealing with powerful people and about dealing with regular folks who gotta deal with powerful people," Clifford continued. The graveness and gravity of his tone and demeanor were enhanced by the deep lines of wrinkle that creased his face. "I know this," he said, "You gotta get people to care to stop this before any plans get under way to start it."

"Think so?" Abe offered very much wanting the advice to come.

"Oh yea. It's damned tough to get folks around here, these hardscrabbled, do-for-themselves folks, to care about something that's already underway. Makes you a whiner can't deal with what's come your way. Now, you show those same hardscrabblers the corruption of the politicians and the rich, well they're more than happy to hear your cause on account they always believe that to be the case and are eager for validation."

Abe was processing what Clifford Blow had said and

only replied, "Uh-huh," though was receptive in tone. Clifford always seemed to know all and foretell all and Abe didn't take it for granted now.

"You gotta show 'em the swindle in this before they try to get a vote goin' or break ground. Folks'll take for granted how something comes to be once its begun, but they won't stand for feelin' like a rich fella, especially Little Jim, is puttin' folks outta home for the sake of business."

"How do I show 'em the swindle?" Abe asked. At this moment, he was mighty grateful for whatever urge had caused him to swing through town for late night coffee and for Clifford sittin' up nights in the coffee shop.

"I know a guy who'd know," Clifford offered. "I ain't exactly the one to figure out who you can trust with that. Take it to the paper or TV station maybe, though they might get it buried in tryin' to uncover the story by talkin' to the wrong people. Joe Dee Miller though, he'd know what to do. He used to make a career outta stoppin' rich folks gettin' over on poor ones."

Abe knew the name, even had a face in mind, though didn't know the man well. "He used to be a defense lawyer and City Judge?"

"That's the one."

"Don't know I seen him around much," Abe said and tried to think if he had. "I seen him years ago. He was the one always had a hippie beard and glasses right? He don't still work at the courthouse does he?"

Clifford of course knew because he knew about everything. "Nah, he got pushed off the bench for being a little too liberal for this area. Started gettin' railroaded in the courtroom otherwise so it made any private practice hard for him. I don't suppose hard drinkin' helped him. He run with a bit of a hippie crowd fer sure." Clifford didn't seem to have any judgment at this. He was simply painting a picture with the details he knew.

"Could he even help then?" Abe's question was fair.

"Don't know really. He works at the high school now—runs the in-school suspension room from what I understand. "

"Oh," Abe replied at the pause.

"But like I said," Clifford added with an air of having the right sense of things, "he made a point outta trying to stop and expose political corruption, especially where the more blue-collar folks was concerned. This was the kind of thing he handled. Surely he's still got a sense of it, or at least could point you in the right direction."

Abe was sold without much convincing. He trusted Clifford. "I suppose I need to find Joe Dee Miller then."

"I think so. Get them papers to him and he'll know how to work 'em against Little Jim. Seems he used to take particular pleasure in representin' Little Jim's workers in civil suits and injury settlements and the like. He'll know how to make your case. And get that shit to him before Little Jim gets back to town. If you ain't got all this public and out by then, well, he won't have a lot of pressure to be gentle on you or yours."

"You know where I can find Joe Dee?" Abe asked.

"I know a few places you can try," Clifford offered. He leaned forward and began to give Abe all he could think on how to get ahold of Joe Dee Miller.

Ike is driving in in the dark. He'd forgotten how dark the highways were down here at night between towns. How the next town comin' glowed orange—a beacon. Though he knew the orange was just a town, not a beacon. It flashed to Ike that things had been going that way for him lately. Flashes of home in the tunnel ahead dissipated by arrival. When he was younger, eighteen or twenty, heck even only a few years before, there was such optimism that everything he would do would be rewarded. Everything else out there offered a beacon of new opportunity. A place to finally start a home. He had no idea about life's accidents or bad habits. That optimism belied the reality that he hadn't been prepared for a lot of things. Made him run so far and fast he found himself on unfamiliar terrain and couldn't see the starting point anymore. He'd been that innocent and now felt himself so tired of experience he wanted the world to stop spinning so he could catch a break.

Travis Spiller didn't seem to be feeling that way. He was married. He had two kids. He worked hard in the oil field and seemed to like his job. Drove a take-home company truck. As Ike crossed the Willis bridge back into Oklahoma he thought about the friend he'd visited that night, whether Travis was as happy as he seemed, whether he himself mighta been too if he'd stayed. It was only the third or fourth time he'd been back to Whitesboro since graduating high school. After his mother divorced his step-dad of all those years and left the farm for a Dallas suburb, Ike didn't think of it as much of a home. The last time he'd really hung out with Travis was the summer before senior year, when they'd been arrested.

The Whitesboro, Texas Police station wasn't finished being built so they took the mugshots in front of the only white-surfaced wall the wood-paneled portable trailer office had—the bathroom door.

They chalk Ike and Travis' names and booking numbers on a little rectangle slate and make the boys hold it chest high while they photograph—frontside then rightside.

Remove the shoestrings, remove the watch, remove the belt, remove the cap and try to hold and hand it off to the booking officer in a way she don't notice the joint tucked inside the band. All accessories in the bag.

They march Ike and Travis down the shorthaired hallway and put them in the detention room with more short carpet and cots and a scabby twentysomething with his head tucked to his chest sleeping sitting-up on one of the cots.

Ike looked around. He wondered if he was a real criminal now.

Of course he hadn't been criminal. Not like the Tulips or Sledges were criminal anyway. He was just young and dumb--stealing a barbeque smoker off the front porch of the hardware store at night.

After that happened, Ike and Travis didn't really run together, just saw each other at school and didn't keep in touch after graduation. So Ike felt uncertain when Travis rang him up. Travis heard Ike was comin' back to town from his aunt whose sister-in-law just happened to live on the Oklahoma side of the lake and work the Oakland Grocery counter with Sara before Sara started at CW herself. Travis called to say they should get together. Ike thought it might be awkward or odd. Thought maybe Travis was in need of some validation. Thought maybe Travis just wanted to show off what he'd got. Or, perhaps it was simpler. Maybe it was just a moment of nostalgia.

Whatever motivated it, it was nothing in the end.

Ike felt nothing toward Travis or his family. They seemed like they were doing nice. They were nice. But Ike didn't know them, didn't know Travis anymore, and didn't feel the energy to even pretend to care. The evening had been a polite dinner and a few beers.

Travis' lovely bride insisted Ike stay and sleep on the couch because of the few beers they'd had. Ike did not see the need as he'd drove after drinking plenty more than that and certainly didn't want to stay. He also didn't want to be rude, so he had agreed to the couch.

Laying on the couch in the dark strange house though, he decided he couldn't take it, probably wouldn't really be in touch anyway, and put his boots on and slipped away while the Spillers slept.

Now, as he drives back north from Whitesboro toward his dad's Oakland lot, he must slam on the brakes. He comes to a harsh stop and his chest pulls against the locked seatbelt hard. A bobcat stands in the middle of the road. Ike is just south of the Willis Bridge, where 377 crosses the lake on into Oklahoma. He can smell the lake water.

The bobcat stares at the Jeep head-on for a moment. Ike wonders what it sees, looking into the bright round lights of the Jeep.

Whatever it sees, it suddenly breaks and sprints straight at Ike and makes an aggressive lunge, at the front of the vehicle, disappearing for a beat. Then it scrambles up over the hood of the Jeep and keeps going. As it goes over the windshield Ike hears its growl and sees its white underbelly. The flat roof of the Wagoneer screeches and pounds and echoes inside the cab as the big cat runs over the top. In the rearview, Ike sees its big back paws push off as it dismounts and continues straight down the highway and out of sight of the glow of the taillights.

After a few seconds, Ike takes his foot off the brake and continues on. His stomach shakes for a few hundred yards.

Crossing the Willis bridge, where his father had stood just hours before, Ike looked into the dark water. He remembered the night, probably the summer before senior year as well, Eric Barton and Tyler Brady had gotten just drunk enough and ballsy enough that they hauled off and jumped off the middle of the west side of the bridge. Ike done bridge jumping. The 901 Bridge off toward Collins-ville south of Whitesboro was a nice twenty foot jump into a twelve or fourteen feet creek. It didn't take being too cra-zy. The Willis though was a good sixty or seventy feet above water at centerpoint. And Ike'd always heard stories from his dad and among others that folks junked and threw off all kinds of stuff in the water from the bridge there. But Eric and Tyler had jumped off that night as crazy as the bobcat'd just charged Ike's Jeep. Eric and Tyler, like the bobcat, made it safely. Ike didn't get up the nerve then.

He imagined none of them would these days.

When he had made most of the journey back to his dad's lot he sees there are flashing yellow lights just around the 377 bend on the way in to the southside of Madill. As he rounds the bend Ike sees a barricade like the ones he'd just seen blocking lanes back up 377 toward the lake, only this one is blocking the little rural residential road that runs the back way into Oakland and skips all of Madill. Ike slows his Jeep, and, as he does so, starts to make out the vehicle behind the road block. It is an old orange GMC pickup.

He'd simply maneuvered through the barricade and detour out on 377 with no workers present and no other traffic, the same way Abe had not long before, unbeknownst to Ike. The road to cut up to his dad's though looked firmly blocked. It had been a time since Ike drove through Madill at night so he decides he doesn't mind the long way through town and accelerates again, past the turn for the residential road and the block and truck. As he passes there is a *whip-crack* noise unmistakable to a .38 snub nose revolver, and Ike turns his head in time to catch the flash of pistol blast and the face it lit. He could swear it was the face of Allie Sledge.

Ike had been in school with the two youngest Sledge brothers—Andy and Randy. The two boys lived then with an aunt on the Texas side during the school year and went to Whitesboro like Ike. Ike figured that was probably because Madill didn't want to mess with any more Sledges after the much older brothers, Shane and Alistair, from what he'd heard of them around his dad's lot. Ike knew the faces of Shane and Allie from his time spent in the small town world of Oakland and Madill. He can't imagine what they were doing or why they'd fire with a car passing. He continued the curve of 377 past the hospital and into the south end of Madill. He went north at the 377-70 Y-intersect and made his way past the main drag businesses, past Hobo Joe's, on out to the north end of town where he took the left turn for Highway 70 for the short jog west to Oakland. He turned off Highway 70 at Nance and then turned back west on Duff before pulling into his dad's driveway.

"You alright?" Abe asked Ike from the living room recliner as Ike came inside. King was sleeping under Abe's footrest until Ike had opened the back door. Now he sat up along with Abe.

Ike was struck by the genuine concern in his daddy's

voice. Abe was mostly reticent if a little hot tempered and jolly at the same time in Ike's image of him. Concerned, not generally.

"Doin' good—why?" Ike tried to be genuine too though also thought it was a real good time to pop a couple more antidepressants for the buzz. He'd begun to wonder where he might get a prescription or score some weed down here when the Chicago doctor's prescribed ninety-day supply was gone well before its refill date.

It was coming on early morning and Ike noted Abe had coffee on, so went to the kitchen galley off the backdoor for a cup. Apparently Abe had done a little more clean-up, though the piled mess remained on the table. Ike took the opportunity to down four Lexapro with his first sip of coffee he'd poured himself before coming back in view of the living room where Abe remained with his fourth or fifth cup of coffee in the recliner. King had put his head down again and shut his eyes—a prisoner in his own home for the second night in a row.

Abe felt he'd let the question hang long enough though Ike hadn't thought of him actually answering.

"Well why is I mighta gotten involved in something with some shitty folks. Impound and druggie shit—" Abe generalized for the moment.

"Yea?" Ike flashed to the pistol blast at the block coming in.

"Sledges actually—if you remember 'em," Abe offered more directly.

Ike was suddenly charged with adrenaline.

"Oh yea—matter of fact—" Ike began before he knew how he might want to say it. "—well I think I seen Allie Sledge comin' in just now. At a barricade on the road comes in the back way to Oakland. Had to take the long way through town.

"Police block?" Abe grew anxious and reached and pulled a cigarette from the pack on the side table next to his coffee cup and lit it.

Ike sat in the padded rocker on the other side of the side table and set his cup down and pulled his tobacco pouch and began to roll his own cigarette as he explained. "No— just an old sawhorse construction orange barricade with a flashin' light. Thought maybe there was a road or powerline crew out there. Then, swear I seen gun fire as I drove by and Allie Sledge behind the blast firin' it."

"Shit," Abe said, more angry now.

"Shit what? Your thing got to do with that?" Ike had more energy in his responses now than earlier in the day.

"Yea—prolly so. They been messin' with me some over that impound—that shitty pickup out there in the lock-up. Shot was likely kinda a warnin' toward you. They shot it up here some last night. Randy and Andy did anyway. The ones about your age."

"How'd they know to look for me to get to you? How'd they know I was back or what I was drivin'?" Ike knew it wasn't so complicated, that they were in such a small world down here, but he needed to fill the conversation and it was about as much as he could come up with.

"Small town," Abe said predictably. "We was at the diner earlier, all the neighbors here seen you pull in earlier and leave when we come back from the diner."

"Well shit," Ike offered and leaned back in his chair after ashing his cigarette.

Abe was surprised by his son's hardened response. He'd watched Ike grow up in pieces so that every time he come back around in summer or during Christmas vacation or the like, Abe would always catch himself treating the boy younger'n he was, not recognizing a hole half year or more had passed since the last time and not rememberin' how much of a lifetime of growin' up can happen in such a short time when you are young. It was a lesson learned before, and, here again, Ike suddenly appeared older to his father.

He still thought of Ike as a kid but thinking on it now, Ike was damned near thirty. He was actually around the age Abe had been when he married Agatha. Only a couple years younger'n than when Abe and Agatha had Ike. Past thirty had been considered old then to have a first kid. Shorty was twenty-three or so when Abe was born. Yet, Abe still didn't imagine his son as old as he himself had been at that age.

He wondered where his son was going. How long he'd stay this summer.

Abe decided he couldn't let the conversation drop for the moment, though he was finally growing tired as long as he'd been without any real sleep, and despite the coffee.

Fortunately, Ike had been turning it over in his head and asked after all, "What exactly happened?"

So Abe again rehashed everything he'd just hashed out with Clifford in the diner. The dog. The attempted shooting of the lock and warning shots at the house. The briefcase and its revelations. Innuendo the Sledges must of had smart enough brains to know it could be valuable. That Clifford had cued him into the lawyer that could take it and know what to do with it. That the lot Ike's granddaddy had deeded to Abe, that Abe'd built his own house and shop and life on, was pretty well at stake.

Abe told Ike too of Joe Dee Miller and the conversation with Clifford Blow. He shared Clifford's plan that public recourse and outcry was the best way to protect everyone in the mean time and save the lot in the long run. Anything else might lead to seizing of the lot, and worse, someone getting hurt or killed in the nonsense.

Ike followed well. His follow-up question was thoughtful: "How long you been here after growing up, the trailer, this house and the shop?"

The question grabbed Abe as he'd been thinking on it himself a lot. "Forty some-odd years now." He said it with reassurance. "That after bein' in six schools by the time I was in fourth grade. One of 'em was a Mennonite one-room schoolhouse even."

Ike knew his daddy had been moved around as a kid. Missouri, Oklahoma, Colorado, back to Oklahoma. Now though he felt new sympathy for it. He'd never thought of it from his dad's perspective at the time—that of a little kid unable to make friends and adjust he was moved so much. Shorty Dyson took the job with his younger brother JL in the Chevrolet House in Madill and finally settled his family. Little Abe Dyson finally had a home and a place to get used to.

Much as Ike had been moving around he could certainly relate to feeling out of place at times. Ike was struck in a way he never had been about the raggedy Dyson lot. It meant a whole lot. After all, it were instinct had brought him now when he'd grown too out of place in Illinois this time around.

"Really think it was just a warnin' shot I seen?" he asked.

"Yea. I don't think they're at the point of knockin' anyone off. They just shot the padlock and brick wall here.

Brought a crossbow even."

Ike laughed at that. Abe smiled too.

"So we gotta find Joe Dee tomorrow," Ike said to move it forward.

Abe was struck his son had drafted himself into the fight by something like grateful relief and fear. In the end, he figured the Dyson boys driving around to find Joe Dee shouldn't be too dangerous, so Abe agreed with his son without thinking too long. "Yea," he said, "we'd better."

The Dyson boys started to watch the TV, first out of the side of an eye, then both became engrossed. *High Noon* was on. Gary Cooper was actin' tough with his pigeon-toed walk.

Ike thought about TV at his dad's. Westerns. The John Wayne all-night marathon. He remembered fondly how his dad liked Woody Wood Pecker and *Looney Tunes* too. Ike's favorites with his dad when he was a kid were *Bonanza* and *The Rifleman*. Him and Abe could agree on TV.

By the time he looked back at his dad as he snubbed out the cigarette he'd slowly and languidly smoked, Abe had joined King in sleep, stretched back in the recliner above the dog.

Ike imagined his dad must not of slept much with all that had happened over the last couple days.

Ike thought it better to snort the pills this time and went in the bathroom to crush several in a line. He came back to the living room and looked at Abe, determined he himself would not sleep, and went to the kitchen and drained the pot to the grounds and started a fresh one. When he returned to the living room he sat on the couch, placed the cup of coffee on the side table nearest the couch's armrest, and rolled another cigarette. He stretched back against the armrest to smoke and listen to the coffee make.

Ike promptly fell asleep with the burning cigarette in his hand. It dropped and burned harmlessly out on the blue shag carpet. The coffee brewed and the full pot scalded for an hour and half before the coffeemaker's electric timer clicked off, the pot untouched as the Dyson boys slept.

GRASS-GROWN TRAILERHOUSES

SUNDAY

When Abe woke his son was asleep on the couch. Abe picked up the half burned cigarette from the carpet and dropped it in the undrunk coffee on the sidearm next to Ike and carried the cup into the kitchen, depositing its contents in the trash and placing the cup in the sink. As he grabbed the coffee can he noticed the coffee maker's full pot, noted too it was cold and silted, and dumped it in the sink before refilling the coffee maker and switching it back on.

When he went in the living room Ike was sitting up, a bit dazed looking.

"Mornin'" Ike managed to offer.

"Mornin'" Abe replied and added, "Nice to get a little sleep." He noted the time on a clock that hung above the TV—it was already nine-thirty. Though he felt a strong urge to converse with Ike, to ask him what exactly he'd been up to in Illinois, how whatever teaching he'd mentioned had been, if that's what he still did, where he was headed, what had made him turn out like he was. Abe Dyson felt too the urge for safety, for Sara, for King, for himself, for Ike. He was more and more convinced as Clifford Blow was that Joe Dee Miller was the key to that safety and the likeliest shot at saving the lot in the process. While he was glad for the sleep, now he felt behind. It seemed like ages since he'd talked to Clifford earlier in the morning, the night before. "I think I need to get a move on—find Joe Dee. Get everything off my plate with this."

Ike was still waking and needed to pee badly. As he stood and walked toward the bathroom he simply replied, "Ok, lemme get my shit together and we'll go."

As he peed Ike realized he didn't have any pills in his pockets. Knowing they must have fallen out into the couch cushions at some point, he grew anxious Abe might see them before he could scoop them back up. He finished off and zipped and went back to the couch.

Abe had gone toward the back door to let King out and followed with a cigarette and cup of coffee to supervise the dog and make sure he come back inside. The pills were tucked under a crocheted blanket Sara had made and Ike must have pulled off the back of the couch at some point in the night. Ike grabbed them and returned to the bathroom.

He downed a few pills, ran water over his face and hair, removed his shirt and applied found roll-on deodorant in a pile of toiletries where the shelf had been shot and fallen, then mouthwashed. Ike came out to the living room to retrieve the calfskin boots. He'd evidently kicked those off at some point in the night as well.

He stepped into his grandpa's boots more easily than the first time. He stooped to grab his tobacco pouch and quickly rolled an ugly cigarette. He headed outside to grab a new shirt from the bag in his Jeep and smoke a cigarette with his dad.

Abe was leaned against the pole of the carport, smoking and watching King chew on part of an old tire. Ike stood shirtless next to Abe and lit his cigarette and returned his lighter to his jeans pocket. "Muggy as hell already," Ike said and tried to feel the cool of the cigarette thinning his blood.

"Goddamned summertime in southern Oklahoma," Abe agreed. He dropped and stomped the butt of the cigarette and snubbed it out with his boot on the concrete of the carport and kicked it off into the yard.

Ike started moving toward his Jeep. He held the cigarette in his mouth while he rifled through his bag and found the lightest shirt he could, a light denim-colored thin cotton pearlsnap. He awkwardly put the shirt sleeves on first while still holding the cigarette and then grabbed the ashy construction from his mouth with his right hand and using just his thumbs to turtle up through the already mostly buttoned shirt. Abe smiled as he watched his son dress. He thought it didn't look all that different than when Ike was a kid, except for the cigarette.

Ike was thoroughly winded having dragged too much smoke in his mouth and lungs on account of holding the sloppy cigarette so prolonged in his mouth. He straightened his shirt with his hands in the morning Oklahoma sun, using the steamy air around him to try and iron the shirt somewhat. His body was already sweaty.

"Lookin' a little like an escaped convict," Abe joked, noting the dark denim jeans and light-denim colored shirt.

"Convicts don't look this damned good," Ike shot back and grinned.

Abe laughed a chortle, entertained by his son's wit. He thought Ike was right too. The shirt was actually a worn, stylish vintage pearlsnap, fit-cut. Despite losing weight, Ike maintained the big Dyson barrel chest and shoulders. To Ike's blessing he'd also reached an average height, 5'10" or 11". Abe had always been an inch or two shorter than his peers and Shorty was called Shorty for a reason, standing all of 5'4", though he'd been handsome too. A full mouth and big brown eyes with a full head of smooth dark hair. Abe thought now how much Ike looked like Shorty, only taller. Same facial features. Abe wondered if he had the same handsomeness himself. His own head was still full of dark hair like his fathers', though he wore his much longer and shaggy, and had maintained a beard in some form or another the last couple of decades, which Shorty never had. Abe also'd had his nose broke twice riding bulls in the regional rodeo circuit in those younger days. His honker had a certain hardness to it that Shorty and Ike's did not. Abe wished his dad was here to stand on the Dyson lot with the two of them so they could all be together a last time. So OE Dyson could see how much his grandson turned out handsome like him.

"Really is a nice old Wagoneer," Abe said, complimenting his son's Jeep again. Cars were always a conversation starter for Abe.

"Yea, couldn't pass up the deal. Just needed some tuning and seat swappin', and those damned water pumps it throwed. Always liked these old Wagoneers."

Abe liked that his son had become a car guy. He always seemed to want a vintage beater over anything new. The same might be said of Abe himself. Ike'd never had trouble picking up the mechanic's trade when he'd worked in Abe's shop during his stays and was generally an enthusiastic audience for automotive history and cars. Abe felt suddenly very grateful his son had always connected with him and his interests. Cars and westerns and history documentaries. Abe wondered how good he really was as a dad at connecting with his son's interests outside of his own. He thought sadly that he probably was not good at that.

Abe Dyson felt another moment of gratefulness that his son was here now.

"Alright—pretty well ready," Ike announced. "Just need a cap. Got one I can borrow?"

Abe hadn't really been a cap wearer though Shorty had. Despite this fact, Abe had collected hundreds of caps over the years. Dozer style, washed style, fitted style, wool, mesh, cotton, flat brimmed, flimsy brimmed, stiff brimmed, bent brimmed, and all. They were stamped and stitched with local business logos and names and services and slogans. Most were a hideous camel by committee print job. Most were pretty obviously dated by style. Abe didn't have a fondness for any of them or the collection really, but maintained them as a steady mountain on the top shelf of his closet, throwing each new one atop the pile and forgetting about it once they were given. Most of the businesses on the caps were now defunct.

"I got a closet full of 'em. Go grab one."

"Thanks," Ike said and threw his cigarette without snuffing it into the yard and walked back inside to find a cap.

Abe figured Ike must have picked up the habit living where there was more rain and less hot sun. He dutifully marched to where the cigarette burned amid the dry brown grass and stomped it casually into the crunchy vegetation of the lawn. He then made a noise something like clicking for a horse to come and King looked up from his chewed tire and came bouncing toward Abe who was turning to go inside as well.

Ike was already in Abe and Sara's room, rifling through the mound of caps in the top of the closet. King jumped on the waterbed rather entitled and plopped down in a fetal position and looked to nap. Ike pulled three caps down and eyed them.

"I think we better go heeled too," Abe said trying to joke as if it was one of the western movies but feeling quite grave at the necessary precaution. He'd attained a few guns over the years besides his grandmother's old Sears and Roebuck double-barrel. He'd even took an interest enough to build a few historic working replicas from bought kits when a History Channel special or thinking on his dad's time in World War II or Uncle JL's time in Korea charged him to do so. He'd hunted a bit before and after his divorce, but hadn't loved it enough to keep going year after year. So there were several hunting rifles in his cabinet that hadn't been fired or cleaned in a minute. He'd never actually been an avid shooter of any of his guns, but when compelled to do so, seemed to do so naturally well.

Ike didn't register the comment much as he narrowed the cap choice to two. The anxiety meds were kicking in and he took an unusual pleasure in selecting his crown. The two were a stiffer black cap that had neat printing for a long since closed transmission shop Abe had done some parts trading with and a washed style brown ball cap that had the simple blue and red and gold logo of the defunct Clint Williams Peanut Company. Ike settled on the latter deciding the brown best matched the worn leather of his grandpa's boots and threw the black cap back up in the top of the closet with all the rest.

"Grab a gun," Abe said as he walked toward the gun cabinet in the other room to make sure Ike was with it and to see how much it unnerved him.

"Okay," Ike said without trepidation though the idea made him as nervous as it made Abe. He went out of Abe and Sara's room to the gun cabinet in the spare room that was once Ike's own room across the hall, where Abe already was, staring at the guns in the cabinet.

Ike realized that the area was still rough country. Lots of shiny new businesses did seem to be springing up of late in Madill. And on the Texas side of the lake a lot of farms and meth lab properties had already been converted into new near lake developments, chopped up and sold in lots for ritzy new homes. Yet a volley of gunfire as told by Abe and still evidenced by the broken bathroom window and shelf and the split in the headboard of the bed in this room hadn't warranted police activity. People of Oakland still weren't alerted to a few shots fired. And Abe himself had decided not to get police involved. Though that, Ike remembered, was well warranted if they were as easily swayed as Clifford had indicated to Abe they might be.

Abe used his keys to open the cabinet and grabbed his .45 revolver again. He wondered why he even bothered to put it back up the day before. Ike remembered the gun as the one Abe had carried in the glove box of the wrecker, in case any impounds involved any hairy situation, like the shootout they'd seen in Buncombe Creek with Danny Tulip Jr. involved. The gun was already loaded and Abe pocketed several more shells then stuck the .45 in the back of his jeans, not really bothering to conceal it under his black t-shirt.

"I'd say grab what's most comfortable," Abe said, knowing his son had grown up shooting guns a couple of times with Abe, often with Lee, and quite a bit on the farm where his mama and stepdad had raised him. Abe went out of the room for more coffee and another cigarette before they were off.

Of handguns there were a few options at Ike's disposal. He began to look them over as thoroughly as he had studied the caps though caught himself and resolved not to take as much time in making the choice. The single shot pre-Civil War replica was out of course. A .38 semiautomatic held some enticement, but ultimately Ike grabbed the awkward 5-shot revolver his grandpa had used as volunteer sheriff's deputy.

It too was a .38 and Ike dutifully stood at the cabinet, filled all five cylinders and, as Abe had, pocketed a handful of shells in case. He put the gun into his back belt but took care to cover it with his shirt.

He hadn't carried a gun that way since a summer before college on his stepdad's farm. There, on occasion, water moccasin infestations would get so bad they had to carry a piece out to the pasture just in case they come across a nasty moccasin or two running across the grass, tank to tank. Ike was about to get lost in the thought of snakes and the farm he grew up on across the lake when Abe asked if he was ready to go.

"Pretty well," Ike said, "just let me get a little more coffee."

While Abe lit another cigarette, grabbed his keys, and waited dutifully on the carport smoking, Ike hustled to his Jeep and grabbed a Styrofoam gas station coffee cup from the console. He poured its swallow of cold and silted coffee onto the ground, went past his dad, and returned within a few moments with the cup full of black coffee.

"I lost the lid so mind your drivin'," Ike joked with his dad, and Abe appreciated the humor though he'd begun to grow quite serious with his thoughts. "Where to first?" Ike asked when Abe did not reply nor react to the coffee joke.

"See if Joe Dee's home, I guess. Bronco's parked out back."

Abe had a habit of parking by the shop's office door since it was usually where he went first when he returned from anywhere though last night he'd parked there habitually when he returned from the diner conversation with Clifford and marched into the house. Ike went for the passenger door of the brown Bronco and Abe let King, who'd followed, into the back of the vehicle before going into the shop. Ike thought of following for a moment, but decided instead to crawl into the Bronco and take the opportunity to roll another cigarette. When Abe emerged a couple of minutes later he was carrying an old brown accordion file folder, grease smudges all over it. Ike had the passenger door open, smoking and drinking his coffee. Without a word, Abe marched over to the driver-side door and crawled up in the Bronco. He threw the closed file folder down on the floorboard behind Ike's bucket seat, in front of where King was laying.

"Let's go," Ike said, suddenly full of energy for the task at hand.

Abe drove the residential way into Madill, neglecting Highway 70 and instead taking short jogs and turns on Duff to Nance to Cedar to Oakland's Main which turned into Lillie Boulevard running over to Madill within a minute and a half drive of Abe's front door. Lillie Boulevard veined through the middle of Madill, mostly a residential road, then on east toward Logan Bird's old dentist office, Busy Bee Dry Cleaner, and the post office among a few other rotating store fronts before it come to the traffic light at the intersection of 377 running north to south through the middle of Madill the other way. Lillie Boulevard ended at the courthouse a block east of the intersection.

There was a mile or so stretch between the last clapboards and trailerhouses of Oakland and the western residences of Madill. This stretch was occupied by a couple of pasture properties and a bigger lot with a house where a widower had lived for years. As they passed the widower's lot Ike noted the ever growing collection. The old man had made a habit over the years of obtaining and orderly parking straight-bodied but engine-locked and rusted classic cars around his house. None looked like they'd been run for three decades or more, which was mostly the case.

"I was thinking about that Corvair you used to tell me about," Ike said as they passed the caryard.

"Yea?" Abe was genuinely surprised his son would remember it. Abe had had a lot of cars growing up. He'd probably rattled them off three or four times to his son in various attempts at conversation over the years.

In high school Abe had worked part time at the same Chevy House his dad and uncle worked in all the time. He made a deal with the used inventory manager to buy some of the scrappier used cars at the dealer auctions on advance salary. Abe'd fix the cars up on his own time, often with tools and parts snaked from the Chevy House's own inventory, drive the cars to school a few days and around town, then sell the car off to a classmate or someone else around, pay back the advance, and pocket the profit, big or small.

The Corvair'd come in to his possession in such a manner. He didn't keep it because he especially liked it or thought it special at the time. It was just that the car was rusty and ragged enough once he got it back from auction that a tuned engine and a coat of wax still wouldn't have netted much past the parts put into it. So, Abe decided to keep it as a beater car for him and his buddies to beat to shit and drive until the wheels come off.

Ironically, it was the car he held in possession longest. He and his buddies did beat it to shit driving it all over the backroads of the county for a year and half until a wheel did come off when it threw a wheel bearing.

"I remember you joking y'all'd always keep a couple of cases of beer up in the front compartment with that rear-mounted motor so it'd always ride smooth and y'all'd always have something to drink."

Abe was surprised further at the detail with which Ike recalled Abe's own teenage years to him. "Yea," he said, masking any surprise in his tone.

"Get this," Ike said almost drifting away, "A buddy of mine up in Southern Illinois, lived 'round Makanda, between Missouri and Kentucky there—" he paused to let Abe picture it and respond.

"Yea?" Abe responded.

"He had a KarmannGhia right? Rear-mount air-cooled motor like a Corvair."

"Of course," Abe said, knowing the Volkswagen model though he was glad to never have had to work on one. No one had owned one around these parts.

"Well, we're gonna go to the river and fish some—it wasn't a nice or cherry car or nothin', just hard bodied and run well enough. We got poles and tackle behind the seats. Naturally, we put the cooler—it was Styrofoam—" Ike held up his Styrofoam cup at Abe and sloshing coffee before continuing, "—we put the cooler with the beer and ice in the front compartment. Just like y'all did." Ike gestured toward Abe with the cup again and sloshed more coffee.

"Yea?" Abe responded again, very much interested now that the story had been brought back around.

"So we get about halfway or more to the lake and my bud realizes he forgot his pipe and we'd brought all this pot too."

"Okay," Abe replied now wondering where his son was going again.

"I had my tobacco and papers but he don't like spliffs or joints." Ike clearly didn't feel the need to be guarded with Abe and Abe was okay with that. "So he's saying the whole trip's gonna be ruined if he can't get a good smoke and relax which was the point anyway.

"I'm tired of him thinking about how to resolve it and offering solutions like punching holes in the side of an empty beer can and using it as a bong so I finally just tell him to turn back.

"Well this more'n doubles our time, right?" Ike stopped here to make sure his dad was still following.

"Yea," Abe confirmed that he was.

"Anyway," Ike continued, "we'd come all the way back and we're on the backroads getting close to the river and suddenly we got flashing lights. County Sheriff behind us."

"Shit," Abe said piqued. He'd pulled the Bronco to the stop at an intersection and looked around to see no cars coming from any direction and drove on through the western residences of Madill.

Ike continued: "Well we're freaking out and my buddy's sliding the weed outta his pocket around into a tackle box with stink bait behind the seat that way at least it'll smell like bait and not weed in the car and it won't be in my buddy's pocket if the deputy intends to search us. My buddy's tryin' to do all this casual so the cop don't see us finicking so much while we pull over."

Abe wonders if 'finicking' is an Illinois word or somewhere from further north. He doesn't figure Ike would've picked it up growing up around here.

"Well we don't say nothing to each other really and the cop comes up," Ike continued, "but he's not just walking up, he's giving the kill sign slashing his throat with his finger and actin' all excitable so my buddy cuts the engine while he's putting his window down.

"The deputy takes off his glasses looking all sorry and says real obliging, 'looks like y'all blew a hose if not the whole radiator,' and points to the front of the car and says, 'There's no steam but it's sure dumpin' buckets!'

We got out and sure enough water was pourin' down from under the front of the car." Ike paused and drank coffee, then brought the story back around again: "Goddamned deck lid of the car hit the lid of that Styrofoam cooler and guess that front compartment wasn't as deep as our cooler cuz it smashed the cooler down and busted the foam on the sides. We didn't realize it when we'd closed it. Then, all that backtracking had melted the ice!"

Abe laughed. It was a good story.

Ike realized suddenly how chatty he'd told the whole thing, that the pills buzzing with the morning nicotine and caffeine were probably making him a little stony. He felt embarrassed in front of his dad, but Abe's follow up distracted him from it.

"Well-what'd you do to shake the sheriff?"

"Oh hell. We showed him what it was and he laughed and had a beer with us. Right there on the back road. Don't think he ever thought of searchin' us or nothin'."

"Just glad to see a couple of good 'ol boys goin' fishin' I suppose," Abe said and smiled.

Abe was glad to think to himself there was still a whole army of young men out there—driving old cars on backroads and drinking beer. Probably mostly smoking pot too, though Abe and his buddies never got very acquainted with that when Abe had been young. Abe done it a couple times and all he ever got from it was tired.

Abe looked at his son now. There was also an army of slightly older young men around. Trying to build their own lots somewhere. Trying to talk their young brides into starter houses, trailers maybe like the one he and Agatha lived in until he built the house.

Abe wondered where Ike was in that spectrum now. What he might be thinking of building. Starting to build someday. Or maybe already was.

Abe took a turn off Lillie and slowed to a crawl within a block. This was where Clifford had told Abe that Joe Dee Miller lived. There was no car in the driveway of the little shotgun house. Abe sat with the Bronco running a minute then pulled into the driveway and killed it.

Ike didn't want to state the obvious, and offered instead, "Well, let's see if he's home anyway."

The Dyson men went to Joe Dee's door and Abe knocked. They stood in silence while no one answered.

Ike let a minute or so pass while he looked around at other houses. No one was out. Sunday morning meant everyone was at church or still just getting around. "Maybe he's at church," Ike said.

"Clifford said he doesn't go to church. Said too if we didn't find him home he'd be at the school or his mama's house over in Sherwood Shores."

Sherwood Shores was a little community of modest homes and trailerhouses, not unlike Oakland, on the lake on the Texas side, just across the Willis bridge.

"Well then," Ike reasoned, "ain't a school day, so I'd say we're driving to Sherwood Shores."

"I'd say so," Abe agreed.

They got back into the Bronco, and Abe wheeled her back out of the driveway and back out onto the road. Abe zigzagged back toward the road that run the back way out of Madill and Oakland and caught it to 377 just before the highway winded back south toward the lake. Within a few minutes they were up to sixty-five miles per hour and out of Madill city limits onto the open highway.

"So, where you been?" Abe asked. It was asked a little more bluntly than he intended, it already being on his mind. No one seemed to be out on the highway either this Sunday morning.

"All over, I guess." Ike said, and laughed a little to himself.

"Where's that? Illinois, I know. You still in school?"

"No all done."

Abe knew his son had finished school in College Station down in Central Texas. Then he'd gone to Illinois to graduate school. Abe hadn't been sure what that entailed, but Ike assured him at the time it would mean he'd be higher paid someday when he became a professor. And, it'd help Ike become a writer, he'd said.

Whitesboro, College Station, Illinois. With each school, Abe's son had moved further away from the daily existence Abe knew. Wanting to be a professor and writer of some sort would sure be different than the mechanics Shorty and Abe'd been. Than the farmer Everett, Abe's grandfather, was.

Ike hadn't really thought to answer the question fully, that his dad was just asking because he'd said something about Southern Illinois before. He noticed his dad seemed to be thinking on it though, and tried to think about how to follow up on the answer a little more while throwing the wet nub of his cigarette out the window.

He could sum it up easy: he went north with a girl, lived with two others after that, he'd taught here and there, and really had no idea now what he wanted to do, even if he'd left home so confidently years ago. "I guess I just been drifting around with some teaching jobs, this girl and that. Was even married for a minute. That's something we got in common. Bad first marriages."

Abe was dumbstruck. His son had never said anything that seemed so adult. Yet, he said it so effortlessly, easy, as if he was already used to the general wear of such things. "Wow, when were you married?" Abe asked his son, concealing no surprise now.

"Oh, that was Chicago," Ike said

Again what he said was so effortless and casual, Abe assumed he wouldn't follow up or try to explain anymore. He wondered if he should press, take the interest, and ask. Apparently Ike'd lived in Chicago.

Before he decided if he should ask anymore though, Ike offered it all up. They were a few miles shy of crossing the Willis Bridge over Lake Texoma, heading back to north Texas, where Ike'd been the night before, where Ike'd grown up when he wasn't staying with Abe in the summer or on a school vacation. As they traveled toward the north Texas pastures where Ike grew up without Abe, Ike told all about what he'd been doing since he left both sides of Texoma here.

Ike told of splitting with the girl he'd moved from College Station to Southern Illinois with after they'd lived in a duplex for a little over a year there. They'd gotten a dog together, a husky, and Ike kept it when they split. The husky died in an apparently bad car accident Ike'd had the year after where he'd spun out on a gravel road driving real drunk one night totaling his car and killing his dog. Somehow—he told his dad and Abe listened rapt—despite being completely ejected from the car Ike'd walked away from that accident unscathed though he'd sure been sorry about that dog. Apparently Ike didn't take a second degree from the graduate school he'd been at there, but did pick up enough experience in an English department to land varying teaching jobs over the years: community college night courses, rural high schools, urban high schools, middle-schools that needed a fill-in teacher for a semester or so. Apparently, in summers, when his teaching stipend from the previous job would run out, Ike'd work manual labor. He'd picked fruit in orchards with migrants in Southern Illinois. He helped install a train scale in the big Chicago railyard. He'd even worked at a used car lot doing basic repair work one summer. Abe liked to hear that. He was glad his son grew up to be a worker. Of course Ike'd helped in the shop and Abe knew Ike had to work on the farm of his stepdaddy's.

Ike got to Chicago because he married the second girl he lived with in Southern Illinois after splitting with the first. They moved to Chicago where she'd been from and married and divorced within a year. Apparently after that Ike went up to Green Bay to see it but saw there was nothing to see and caught on with a hobo work crew and ventured all the way out to Billings where, again, he worked in a railyard as temporary labor. After the hoboing he drifted back to Southern Illinois and taught out the school year in Cairo, Illinois, where the Ohio and Mississippi Rivers collide.

Ike told all like it was rehearsed, though it hadn't been. It was eight or nine years of rentals and girls and job to job. He'd totaled three cars. The one that killed the dog when he was drunk. An icy highway in Chicago one morning was the next. An icy bridge in Wisconsin one night was the last. Ike confirmed that he did write stuff every once in a while. Articles and little stories, mostly as a hobby. A couple had been published in little literary magazines.

Now, Ike was back from the Southern Illinois teaching job, though he didn't offer his dad a reason why he was compelled to come back home after all. He offered no explanation of what he was thinking of doing next.

As he was finishing the story of his travels Abe felt bad for his son, though he didn't know if he was supposed to or not. Abe had had road trips and adventures but hadn't been a rambler since his dad had moved his little family around all those years before landing in Oakland. Abe was a fourth grader then. Abe wonders if his son felt out of place, without home, the way he himself so often had at a young age. He was hit with a burst of generosity, wanted to offer his son a place at his lot, the home he was so grateful to have been settled at for so long now, even if it was currently under the assault of Little Jim Canaan's enterprises.

Abe didn't make the offer though. It would have been from generosity. From love. Even from like. He liked the man his son seemed to be. He was good to talk to. He thought they could bond. He didn't want to be forward or out of place though. He didn't know what Ike was feeling. He thought offering him a place on the Dyson lot might be taken as saying he was failing at whatever it was he was trying to do.

For his part, Ike didn't know what he wanted to do, let alone how to begin to get there. This thought struck him as he finished telling of his rambles, just as his dad was thinking on the very same kind of thoughts.

"Well, I don't know what you like writing about, but sure sounds like you got a lot of good details for some stories," Abe said, thinking it was the best thing he could offer. And Ike sure had been doing some interesting stuff. It seemed anyway.

"That's probably true," Ike said, and smiled, and felt better and suddenly realized how easy talking with his dad was. He was glad for that and rolled another cigarette.

"Roll me one of them too," Abe said. Ike complied. He handed Abe a well rolled cigarette, one end narrowed so all the tobacco didn't suck through without a filter. "Like I said, I ain't even gonna ask how you got so good at rolling these," Abe joked again and smiled.

"Well then I ain't gonna tell you how I can," Ike said joking back again as well. He lit his cigarette and shared his lighter with his dad so Abe wouldn't have to hunt his out of his pocket while he was driving.

As he got his cigarette lit, Abe saw the turn for Sherwood Shores, and slowed to make the left. They'd crossed to the Texas side.

As Abe thought of where Ike had been, where he might be headed, how he'd grown up working in both places he was raised, both sides of the lake, it occurred to him that Ike's stepdad's farm was pretty close to where they were at the moment.

"Your step-daddy's family farm ain't too far from here

is it?" Abe asked to make conversation with his son.

"Ex-step-dad," Ike reminded Abe.

"Yea."

It was true. Gordonville was a little settlement small-er than Sherwood Shores by half and just a few miles south down 377. Since Ike's former step-dad's family spread was just west of the highway a couple miles north of Gordonville, it wasn't too far away at all.

"You wanna go by and see it after we find Joe Dee?" Abe asked his son, remembering Ike had said something about wanting to see the mural at the Madill post office. Maybe that's what he was doing back here. Touring the plac-es of his youth, of his growing up.

"Nah, not really," Ike returned, which was true. He'd get around to it eventually, maybe, but it had to wait for now.

The Honeymoons, his step-dad's family, and their farm had soured for Ike long ago.

He thought about the time he burned down his step-dad's dead brother's trailer on the property.

Ike was headed for that crash long before the brakes locked and the handlebars jerked rigid and useless to the right. That old model three-wheeler just kept careenin' straight at the singlewide that rotted on the back lot.

Ike knew at the time that his stepdaddy would put it on Ike drivin' too damned fast and not ever payin' enough damned attention.

But that crash was destiny fulfilled. That crash was a goddamned allegory.

Ike's stepdaddy's brother who had polio and swollen feet had moved the trailer on the back lot years before after his wife left him and he tired of tryin' to live normal. He drank a lot of Old Milwaukee and put a lot of water on his heart and died after he crashed down in the hallway of the trailerhouse comin' out of the shitter one morning.

Weeds and pasture grass had grown up around the trailer since.

The brother died a few years after Ike's stepdaddy's daddy died. The father got some time to yap before he passed and on his deathbed swore Ike's stepdaddy's second family wasn't never gettin' none of his family's farm. Ike and his momma crashed the old man's notion of family bonds of blood.

So Ike knew he might have to burn it all down one day to spite the old sonofabitch.

Ike Dyson bailed before the old Honda three-wheeler hit the trailerhouse broadside and boomed and smoldered and burned.

Ike stood on the back lot and watched the dead cripple's trailer flame.

Of course Ike's stepdaddy never knew the pleasure Ike got out of watching that trailer burn. He'd been an okay stepdad, though Ike never really got past the time he'd said to Ike that he was surprised, "Your mother don't kill you one of these times." That meant he knew it was rough for Ike. It also meant he wasn't going to do anything about it.

Ike thought about when he would visit his mom, his stepdad. He didn't feel angry or resentful toward it all anymore. When he thought about it, the whole lot of them, his mom, his stepdad, his dad, had all been about his age or younger when Ike'd come along.

He couldn't imagine he'd be perfect as a family man now. No reason to expect they should have been better at it then. Nor could he blame them their addictions. He'd been an addict for a long time now. He wasn't a boozer as they were, but he popped pills and smoked more than anyone's fair amount of weed. He'd eaten a variety of psychedelics over the years and would do so again.

Ike's only real nobility over any of his folks was that he didn't have a child witness yet. He'd barely let women witness.

Ike knew his dad didn't know fully the truth of how he'd grown up. The alcoholism. The abuse. How angry and volatile his mom and stepdad became.

For a long time Ike wished his dad would've done more to take him. To keep him. For a long time, he wanted to tell Abe Dyson all the things Ike Dyson had had to grow up with.

Now though, he didn't think it fair to burden his dad with it, especially with all he'd come back to find Abe dealing with. For now, he was riding with his dad, quite comfortable.

There would be time, if he chose, to talk with his dad, to see his mom and her new husband and their house in the Dallas suburbs, to track down his ex-stepdad who'd jumped farms and states and lived on a spread in southeastern Oklahoma somewhere with a woman he'd met at the bar.

"I think Joe Dee's mama's trailer should be somewhere near the water. At least, I was told it was in one of the lots on the lake." Abe broke his son's remembering with the general announcement. They'd made it to Sherwood Shores, turning off 377 just south of the Willis bridge to the residential routes that meandered toward the lake, now heavily scenting the air.

"Well there's only fifty-five trailers on the lake out here," Ike said, joking and having gone to Sherwood Shores often growing up around there. Indeed, he'd probably been in Sherwood Shores more in his life than Abe had in his. "We can check 'em all." Ike was smiling at his own sarcasm.

"Hers is supposed to be pink as all hell from what Clifford says," Abe said and smiled back to his son.

"Well. Hell. There it is." Ike said this without sarcasm.

Abe looked where Ike was looking and braked immediately. Indeed there stood a pink trailer up and to the left. It had a six-inch-high pink plastic picket fence all around the border of the lot's yard. "What's the box say?" he asked though noted with the way his son squinted in an effort to answer that his son's eyes might not be better than his own.

"Not sure," Ike said, confirming such was the case. He couldn't make out the letters even from their short distance in the Bronco's cab. "Print's too small. Pull in," Ike commanded.

Abe did turn the Bronco into the pea gravel driveway attached to the trailer's lot, but just to its edge so they could read the little tag welded on top of the mailbox at the end of the drive. The back of the Bronco was just out of the edge of the road and Abe stopped. The two Dysons could clearly see "MILLER" printed on the mailbox's welded tag.

"Might as well pull all the way in," Ike suggested suddenly leading the expedition.

Abe complied again and nudged forward until he'd pulled two feet or so behind the two-tone maroon and gray Lincoln Continental with gold trim and gold spoke wheels parked under the open carport. Abe noted the model was twenty years or so old but very well kept.

No other car was parked there. It seemed unlikely then that Joe Dee was here either. But perhaps the old woman would know where to look for her son.

The Dyson boys got out of the cab, politely closing their doors. They were dealing with an old lady here and both seemed automatically reserved and quieted their movements in concert.

They gently walked across the lawn from the driveway to the steps leading up to the small deck around the trailer's front door.

The grass was shaggy. Abe's workboots and Ike's grandfather's ropers left distinct impressions as they made their way.

The two cautiously but deliberately climbed the three steps to the wide railed landing. The deck was not covered and the metal of the trailer already radiated the summer sun's heat.

Abe paused and thought about Joe Dee Miller's mom—he wondered how with it she was. If she'd really know where her son is. He hated to bother people.

Ike wasn't eager to talk to an old woman either. He also wasn't eager to hang around on the porch sweating. He knocked on the frame of the storm door when he saw Abe had not moved to do so. The knocking made a noise like a metallic rattling that turned into an echo down the corrugated tin sides of the trailer that sounded almost like a laser beam being fired.

No one answered.

When a minute and half or so had passed Abe finally offered the most obvious: "She ain't here or can't hear us."

"Yea," Ike agreed and turned toward the road. From the porch they stood on he could see a guy about his age walking from the lot of the trailer across the road toward him and his dad.

As the guy got closer and Ike could make out his face, the man gave something like a defeated half-smile.

"Howdy," Ike said, greeting the comer before Abe did. He felt he should since he felt he'd spotted the guy first.

"Ain't gonna be anyone home," the guy offered once he was halfway across the yard of the pink trailer, having simply stepped over the tiny plastic pink picket border. Though he neglected to return greeting, he was not unwelcoming in his tone.

"Yea?" Ike asked.

"Yea—actually, Mrs. Miller just passed." The guy was fairly unemotional about this. Ike concluded the guy must have already taken on the task of letting others who maybe had stopped by know of Mrs. Miller's departure. At least he didn't seem disturbed by having to do it now.

Abe felt defeated. It was heavy news and didn't really offer any room to ask anything else. The guy spoke again though, unprompted.

"In fact, her son's just drivin' back from burying her back up north. Called this mornin' askin' me if I could do some mowing for him over here on account he won't be back today to get to it."

"Yea? When's he back?" Ike asked, grabbing the reigns again, taking advantage that this guy—who was seeming increasingly familiar to Ike—knew Joe Dee Miller.

"Says tomorrow—he runs a summer school program of some sort over at the high school in Madill. It's where he lives," Mrs. Miller's neighbor added, nodding in the direction of across the lake.

Abe thought of Clifford Blow, how he was always

right as rain. If he was speaking it to someone else it was somehow always the truth. So apparently it was the case that since being removed from the county court defense Joe Dee was working as a part-time administrator of sorts at Madill High School.

"Shit—guess that'd be as good a place as any to catch up with Joe Dee," Ike said, also thinking on Joe Dee's job at the high school, turning from the neighbor to Abe.

"Sure—except it's a whole 'nother damned day," Abe said, listless. He wanted to get everything to Joe Dee as quickly as possible. He'd been a little uncertain at first of Clifford's plan, but once he convinced himself it was probably the best course of action he'd felt a certain calm in that decision. At least it involved getting rid of the contents of the briefcase which were all that threatened him and his family. And now, on Sunday morning, he felt an extreme urgency to execute. To be rid of the contents of the case. To put them in the hands of the man that could get them to the right channels to expose the corruption behind the highway deal to stop it in its tracks. So Abe could keep his lot. It was all swirling heavy in his brain.

He and Ike said nothing else of their disappointment. The guy had been nice to let them know, but he didn't need to know why they needed to see Joe Dee.

"I know you right?" the guy asked looking at Ike.

"I've been thinkin' that," Ike confirmed but added, "though couldn't place it."

"Keith Topper," the guy said.

Ike recognized him now. He'd been in elementary and middle school with Ike then drifted off somewhere else in high school. Ike realized now he'd never thought of him once he left. He didn't know if he'd switched high schools or just dropped out all together as he thought of it now.

What he did know was that Keith Topper—as Ike himself had been—was chubby as a kid. Like Ike now, Keith Topper was quite skinny, though Keith Topper looked much rougher than Ike. Where Ike simply looked tired and had the few wrinkles that came with such a look, Keith's face looked to be in the beginnings of decay. Where Ike still had broad shoulders and a broad chest and muscle to his arms, Keith simply had straight lines and looked fairly weak if anything. All of this was made painfully clear as Keith Topper now wore no shirt. Only jeans and no shoes.

"Yea, we were in school together at some point," Ike confirmed before letting too much time pass.

"Yea, 'til I left school after eighth grade," Keith Topper said, and grinned a grin of rotten teeth. Ike thought he must have been on and off meth at some point.

"Yea, I remember that," Ike said making small talk, now just wanting to leave with his dad.

"I hardly recognized ya," Keith Topper continued. "You lost so much weight. You was chunky like me in school."

Ike thought it was funny how, whatever the paths they'd taken to get to the dead Mrs. Miller's front lawn, he and Keith Topper had about the same reaction in seeing in each other. "Yea, you lost the weight too," Ike said, and half-grinned. "We better get on, don't ya think, Dad?" Ike asked and turned to Abe again, very much ready to leave.

Abe felt the same about it and relieved his son. "Yeah, we need to get back. We're obviously not gonna talk to Mrs. Miller, but we got what we came for. We know where we can find Joe Dee next. Thank you, Keith," Abe said, turning from Ike to Keith and not wanting to be impolite.

"No sweat," Keith Topper said, again with his half-defeated smile. "Tell Joe Dee I got to his mom's lawn." Keith looked around at the shaggy lot, and added, "I'm gonna do that later this evening, give it a chance to cool off."

"Will do," Ike replied for both he and Abe and added, "Good to see you Keith. Take care of yourself."

"Will do," Keith Topper said in ape.

Abe and Ike walked back to the Bronco, crawled in, and Abe backed out and onto the road again.

"Go on up instead of the way we came in and you can come out on 377 closer to the lake, by Juniper Point." Ike was still leading the expedition and had been around Sherwood Shores more than Abe so Abe complied and continued across the road they come in on off 377, straight ahead as Ike had suggested.

At the next intersection of the rocky roads that paved Sherwood Shores, roads much like the curbless cracked streets of Oakland, Abe paused at the intersection. No cross traffic was coming. He knew which direction to go. Yet he did not take his foot off the brake. He did not accelerate or move. He stared at a trailerhouse, green and white and rusted, cattycorner from where he and Ike sat in the Bronco.

This was Danny Tulip's trailer.

Abe looked at the Tulip trailer that was more than the Tulip trailer. It'd once been the Dyson trailer. Where Abe and Agatha lived before and just after they'd married when Shorty Dyson had give his son the south half of his wooded lot in Oakland.

Abe traded motor work and an RV he'd restored some for the green and white singlewide trailerhouse and nestled it on a ridge in the Dyson lot between oak, pecan, and persimmon trees. He'd thought it well accomplished at the time but Agatha never agreed and was always apprehensive at being stuck in a trailerhome long term. Once he'd built the house he sold the trailer to Danny Tulip, who moved it over here to Sherwood Shores for his little family.

Ike looked at his Dad and thought of the same narrative. He'd heard it in pieces from both parents and pieced it together pretty well.

Of course, his brain flashed on Benny Tulip. This was his stony mind—it would always jump back to things his sober brain never seemed interested in. Random things from school or his childhood. When he thought of them at times like these, when he could feel his buzz and it eased his anxieties, the things his brain thought back to seemed so vital and important, even if he hadn't thought about them for a long time.

As Ike looked from his dad back to the abandoned and grass-grown trailer, he thought of the time Benny Tulip pushed him and almost broke his brain.

Ike went to school with Benny since the Whitesboro school district ate up the rural community of Sherwood Shores.

Ike Dyson had been sittin' on a schoolyard fence.

Benny Tulip comes walkin' up and puts a flash of the green and white trailer in Ike's head—the one he'd seen in a couple of Polaroids.

As Ike knew it Ike's dad had to talk Ike's mom into the til-we-have-a-family-to-save-money trailer cuz she swore she'd never be trailer trash.

Ike's folks sold the trailer once Ike was conceived there and his mother swore she'd burn it down before she'd be there and be fertile. Ike's folks sold the trailer to Benny's folks who too just conceived a son. Their second.

Benny Tulip was raised in a trailer of disdain.

Benny got hit. Benny got shot. Benny stole a car. Benny got taken from his folks. Benny got fostered with the weird smelly lady science teacher. Benny wore donated shoes everyone'd all already seen in the church clothing-drive bin. Benny got hardknocks.

Benny pushed Ike off that rail that day for all the horrors of his life.

Ike Dyson felt his head concave and convex as the concrete first dented then swelled his gourd.

Benny wants to cover his ass and swears at everyone gathered to see that it was all a joke and, whether it is or it ain't, Ike Dyson gets it.

He got it then and he gets it now. Ike wonders where Benny Tulip is now.

Ike's brain switched back to the thought of his parents in the trailer, before Benny Tulip had such a horrible life in it. He knew they hadn't stayed in the trailer long once Agatha was pregnant. This was despite birth control as Ike eventually learned it when his mother told it to him with a wine buzz when he was thirteen or so. Agatha was bragging at the time to her son how she'd pushed, despite Abe's lack of ambition, to apply for a government program to borrow low and pay longterm and build a home. She'd pushed Abe to give up his welding job in Madill and drive to work at the tire plant in Ardmore every day. They had a kid to build a home for, and by-God, Agatha was the one that'd made it all happen. She'd said.

Ike knew his mom had overcome a lot growing up.

It was why her anxiety to push often overtook all else. She'd been the dirt poor daughter of Dust Bowlers and it made her push to never return to harder days, no matter how far she got from them.

Abe was thinking on nearly the same thing. How he'd cleared a few trees from his half of the Dyson lot, attaining a massive outbreak of poison ivy for which he spent a day in the hospital it swelled his eyes and balls so big. He measured out the middle of the property after moving the trailer house to the far west side with a borrowed one-ton rig from a friend. Then, he poured a concrete slab and worked like mad to build a little brick house for his little family. And though his wife had protested because she didn't want those junky cars to stack up, Abe even finagled it to build a modest tin building for a shop to take in side work as mechanic or maybe even restore an old car or two for himself one day. The house was finished a few weeks before Agatha gave birth to Ike, a few weeks overdue on Thanksgiving Day. The shop became an ever expanding enterprise for Abe, and, eventually, his livelihood. The marriage ended within a couple of years of moving in to the house.

All this time Abe knew his daddy'd be leaving the north end of the lot soon—he was headed back to Dewey County in Northwest Oklahoma to retire and run the family farm there. Shorty'd wanted Abe to move his new family with him and Abe's mom. But Abe was compelled to stay. He'd been all over with his dad before fourth grade, chasing job after job. Missouri, Oklahoma, Colorado, Oklahoma again. Abe'd been in six schools before Madill, two in that dusty northwestern plain. One Mennonite school where Abe was the only unmennonite and an Indian school where Abe was considered very white, though he could claim a quarter

Chickasaw since all the Dyson brothers, his uncles and pop, were half on account of Abe's full blood short little native grandmother.

When Abe's uncle, JL, a part-time southern Baptist preacher landed a new parish in Oakland and a job as body man at the Chevrolet House in Madill, Shorty followed his younger brother and was hired as a fulltime mechanic at the Chevy House with JL. Shorty eventually signed on as volunteer sheriff's deputy with Marshall County as well. And there they'd been twenty-five years or so before Shorty got the itch to finally go home to Dewey County in Northwestern Oklahoma.

But Madill was Abe Dyson's home, and he'd never even lived in the agreed up Dyson family seat of Dewey County. So, though he'd spent part of nearly every day with his daddy until he was thirty and a father, he continued with his first wife's insistence to build a house and stay.

Now it'd been forty some-odd years. Shorty had been gone fifteen or more of those.

Abe's boy was grown up, though without the aging milestones of a child around constantly once the divorce took and Agatha took Ike to live with his new stepdaddy north of Whitesboro on a small Texas farm, Abe had found it difficult to pinpoint events over time. He'd expanded his shop onto the north end of the lot. He'd acquired that from his father, and long since had Shorty's blessing to bulldoze the little clapboard house that was the Dyson home of many years. Once Abe quit his factory job at Uniroyal Tire in Ardmore, he'd opened the shop fulltime and slowly built on when he could.

A big boon to the building project was Sara. Sara had spent ten years or a little more working at CW in the hot warehouses doing steel inventory control. She could get sheet metal and tin and whatnot at a discount and soon Abe's original tin-colored tin one-stall shop was a mostly white-tin-paneled four-stall operation with two lifts.

As he looked at his family's starter-home trailerhouse, driven miles from where he'd occupied it, Abe thought about property and the taking of property.

Oklahoma itself had been snatched from Indian Territory a few years after Indian land hand been snatched all over and they were rounded up there. White settlers here got their start running and just taking land, literally. They took lots of property for the big lake later on. Buried all of Woodville, Oklahoma in a flood of red water. Snatched farm land to house Nazis POWs they used to clear the land and damn the river to build the lake. Snatched land to build Highway 377 to get to the lake—other roads and bridges around the area and all over really were built on snatched property. Roads Abe Dyson had run all his life.

Abe wondered now if maybe he didn't have the right to keep his land after all. But he kept coming to one piece of nagging nostalgia—the lot was his first home. It'd been so for four decades after the first decade of his life was spent on the road. It meant something to him.

"What's next?" Ike asked.

Though both Dysons recognized the trailerhouse, though it stirred much in both of them, though they'd been sitting in the still vehicle for many moments, neither wanted to discuss it now. Abe was glad his son moved it along for the both of them.

"Well back to the house I guess. Can't make today tomorrow," Abe answered in reply.

"Sure can't," Ike agreed and hung his arm out the

window as Abe turned left and toward the highway on the road Ike'd intended when he brought them this way. They came out on the highway right near the bridge as Ike said they would and crossed back over to Oklahoma.

"You think the Sledges'll keep comin'?" Ike asked his dad when they were a few miles out of Madill.

"Hard to say." Abe was fairly reticent in tone though this was his biggest fear from the moment young Keith Topper had broke the news that Joe Dee wasn't back until morning. Soon as he could get rid of what the Sledges wanted, sooner they'd back off. Sooner Abe could be sure nothing dumb or dangerous was going to happen. "All the same," he added, "we'd probably act like they will and be relieved if they don't."

"Agreed," Ike replied.

King remained restful in the back. He'd barely budged from his spot in the back. He hadn't asked to get out when they'd stopped at Joe Dee's house or Joe Dee's mom's trailer. He hadn't budged when Keith Topper come up.

Sure enough there were Sledge vehicles in the drive of the shop—the Scout and the orange GMC pickup. The four Sledge brothers plus Danny Tulip Jr. and two other rough looking boys stood around their trucks in the gravel lot, holding shotguns and pistols. Seven in all.

Abe stayed at the intersection of Fifth Avenue and Nevins, one block off the higway, the way he and Ike'd come back, his foot on the brake.

From the cab of the Bronco, Abe and Ike could see everything clear. When Abe looked to Ike, Ike'd already reached back and pulled his revolver. Abe thought for a moment.

The Sledge vehicles were parked on the gravel drive

that came off Fifth Avenue and down toward the shop—just shy of where the gravel lot ended and Abe's patchy brown backyard began. The pickup was parked in front of the Scout, both perpendicular to the road. It was a couple hundred yards from the hood of the Bronco leading the Dyson boys and King to where Shane and the Sledges stood.

"Put it down," he said suddenly to Ike.

Ike was struck by the authority in his dad's voice. It was one Ike hadn't heard since he was a little kid. Even then it was rare for Abe to take such a tone. He lowered the revolver to his knee though never let go the pistol grip.

Abe didn't want a shootout. He'd run Andy and Randy off fine before. But they'd been drunk and it was dark and they never seen Abe coming. As hardened as Ike appeared to have become, as ready as he seemed to fight something, more than Abe, Abe still felt the need to protect his son—keep him safe. And the dog of course.

He eased off the brake and rolled on down Fifth, gave a wave out the window which only Shane Sledge returned, pulled alongside the Sledge vehicles, then turned toward the little concrete pad by the shop's office door. He put the Bronco in park and killed it.

"Stay here a sec," Abe said as he used to tell Ike to sit in the cab of the tow truck while he'd go and scope the scene of a wreck or impound and didn't want Ike in the way of the cops or troopers or ambulance or fire or whoever. Ike never got out until all was clear and only the vehicle was left to tow. Then he was free to crawl from the cab and help hitch it up.

Ike didn't intend to stay in the cab this time, though did put the gun back in his belt under the back of his shirt. He rolled up his window as Abe did, and crawled out of the cab with his dad. They shut their doors and turned toward the Sledges at the same time.

Abe'd made sure not to let King out of the Bronco despite the dog's efforts at worming out alongside Abe.

"Where's the briefcase Abe Dyson?" Shane shouted across the lot as Abe and Ike walked toward the Sledge crew. Shane knew well that the young guy with Abe would be Ike since he'd heard through the grapevine Abe's son was back in town running around in a Jeep and had been the one to sic Allie on Ike the night before, to startle Ike into telling his dad to give the case back. As Shane looked at Ike now he saw a man that, like Abe Dyson, probably didn't scare easy. Still Shane was confident—he had Abe outmanned and gunned pretty well.

"Bottom of Lake Texoma." Abe replied honestly as he got near to Shane and the rest and stopped.

Shane figured that quick enough and snorted and replied, "Ok—so where's all the shit was in it? Don't give two cents 'bout the case really." Shane'd been fingering and tapping the pistol butt at the front of his pants. He was the only one without gun in hand but was making sure to keep close reach of it.

"Well that's trickier," Ike interjected and surprised everyone at this point.

Randy, Andy, and Allie had been standing rather stoic and quiet for them. Abe thought Shane had probably warned and threatened them to just be quiet and stand there. Danny Tulip Jr. behaved similarly and Abe concluded the same had been told him. The other two only seemed to half pay attention, their shotguns on their shoulders. One of them wasn't wearing a shirt. Everyone, including Abe, looked to Ike when he spoke up.

Abe felt panic without a clue as to Ike might say next.

Ike himself didn't have a clue as to what he might say next. He had only felt a rather natural impulse to match Shane's contrary mannerisms. Now he badly wanted to snort a row of something that would take away the nerve in him.

He felt awkward a beat later when natural timing had passed and still nothing came for him to say.

Then Ike and Abe and all were jarred as the sudden squall of balding tires and the roar and rattle of a big engine behind them came charging hard.

The Dyson boys turned to look while the Sledge clan looked up and past the Dysons to see Stinkyfoot hauling ass down Fifth off the highway, Lee Wild Child Pitchman at the wheel.

Wild Child blew through the cross of Fifth and Nevins and kept roaring down the road toward the shop's drive where the Sledges had parked. Suddenly he pulled off the skinny road down the grassy shoulder that embanked the west end of Abe's lot shy of the driveway. Gravel was flung as Lee and Stinkyfoot bounced off the grass shoulder into the lot and kept accelerating. He swerved and his contraption of a truck looked near to tumble as he drove around Abe's Bronco. But it didn't, and Lee and his truck came straight for the whole bunch, all four of Stinkyfoot's paws flinging rock and dust.

Abe and Ike dove out of Wild Child's way first.

Evidently Allie and Randy and Andy had a notion to fire a few shots at Lee through the windshield but hadn't raised in time and now dropped their pistols as they rolled and tumbled out of the way.

Danny Tulip Jr. and the other two made a similar show with the same results—their shotguns on the ground, them scrambling every which way.

Shane Sledge was the only one that managed to side-step the calamity with some grace. He remained upright to watch the entire thing.

Wild Child kept the hammer down and used the great pushguard he'd custom built and welded to the front of Stinkyfoot years before, all of the '54 Ford's cab's forged steel, the heavy frame and suspension of a 4x4 Blazer, and the big block under the hood to smash the Sledge Scout broad-side and push it off the gravel into Abe's yard and crunch it against a great pecan tree that stood near the worn walkway from the house to the shop. Glass exploded everywhere and the removable hard top popped off of the Scout and came back down in place. The rest of the old Scout hot-dogged under the strain.

Wild Child, apparently as unscathed as his massive truck, promptly bailed out, wielding a nice little Army issue pistol pointed straight at Shane. The Scout's engine spilled liquid at the base of the tree.

Ike'd recovered enough to pull and hold his grand-pa's gun on the Sledge associates while scrambling toward and standing over their fallen shotguns. Abe managed to his feet and felt the need to pull his gun as well though did not feel as smooth in drawing it as Lee and his son appeared to. Abe took the leftovers and pointed in the general direction of the three younger Sledge brothers before they could scramble back to their guns. If Abe hadn't made him keep his gun hol-stered, Ike realized, he'd have dropped his too.

Dust swirled and mixed with smoke and steam from the busted Scout to create a hot and putrid air around the whole scene.

Shane realized he was outdrawn though despite the excitement had regained the same composure and continued to fondle the butt of the pistol in the front of his pants without any real intention of pulling it now. Instead he offered in his usual calm and callous tone, "Lee Pitchman you gonna put yourself in this now too? Not smart."

"What ain't smart is any intention of harm you got to any of us. Fixed it so." Wild Child said this with great certainty.

Abe now how no idea what Wild Child would say next.

"The hell ya talkin' about Wild Child?" Shane asked as curious as Abe.

Fortunately Lee had more of a plan that Ike had had before: "Well see Abe here enlisted me with what you want and I got it deposited."

"Deposited?" Shane had as little clue as Abe or Ike what Lee was saying.

"Took all the contents of the case, got notarized and certified copies." Lee was taking great pleasure in reciting the official words he'd rehearsed with Clifford an hour or so before in the diner. He continued with the plan as practiced: "They're deposited in a safety deposit. Anything happens to me or a Dyson, lawyers done been entrusted to reveal contents. Includes a notarized letter of documentation of Sledge harassment. A log of you messing with Abe on account of legitimate impound. They'll come for you first, Shane. It's all *notarized*," Lee added on again emphasizing the official word again and smiling. His worn cowboy hat was off his head dangling from the back of his neck from the leather tie-string that fastened to both sides of the worn and curled brim. He still had his Army issue pointed at Shane.

"Well God-damned," Shane uttered, dragging out the swear, looking down defeated. He'd felt so close to his endgame only moments before. Now it seemed there wouldn't be any real way to worm money out of this. If Lee'd been as clever as all that or just was lying out his ass, other folks already knew and would quickly start to connect the case contents to the Canaan house robbery and arson. He didn't need people to think on it. Discuss it. Connect it back to him.

It'd started as simple extortion—hold the case 'til the highway deal started to go public and then make Little Jim Canaan pay big so folks didn't know all the backdoor dealing involved and get riled to stop the build.

"Goddamned is right. Why don't you pile your dogs in the back of the truck and git on," Lee said still feeling very in charge.

Abe didn't let it go at that though. "Whatever I do with that stuff," Abe told Shane, "I can keep y'all out of it if I know y'all have left it alone. No one needs to know how I come by it, officially."

At this Lee and Ike both seemed a little stunned.

"Hell, whatever happens now, shit's more of a liability than a payday," Shane replied unwilling to admit defeat.

"You're probably right there," Abe conceded and did agree.

"Can we get our truck?" Allie asked from behind Shane rather bluntly and nodding toward the shitty truck with the camper in the impound lot that had started everything.

Abe simply laughed and looked down and then back to Shane.

"We're gone Abe," Shane said having only ever cared about saving his blackmail which was now lost. "Load up," he commanded and the other Sledge brothers and Danny Tulip Jr. and one of the two strangers walked toward the orange

GMC like dogs called to take a ride. Like dogs, most hopped in the back. Shane climbed in the driver's side, Alistair the passenger.

The shirtless kid remained a moment then took a step toward the sawed-off he'd dropped in the scramble out of Lee's way. Ike was still paying attention and pointed his 5-shot squarely at the kid's bare chest. "Leave it," he said, and nodded the roughneck toward the pickup with the others.

The kid looked to protest, saw Shane nor anyone else in his crew was paying attention to gathering guns and decided to turn and walk away. He crawled it the truck bed as well.

Shane fired the pickup up and Abe thought the old small block 350 under its hood sounded pretty sturdy still. Without the Scout parked behind now, Shane just backed up the drive and onto Fifth and then went south a half block past Abe's house and lawn, then east on Duff and was out of sight.

The Scout remained against the tree, dripping it's liquids now rather than pouring.

"Banks'll of been closed since noon yesterday," Abe said walking up to his old friend. "Where would you get a safety deposit box today?" Of course, Abe didn't need to ask questions knowing Lee never had anything of the case contents.

"Don't matter. Shane knows people know." Lee seemed rather calm now for all the excitement he'd created.

Ike was busying himself with the collection of the guns which lay scattered. He was careful to empty chambers and put on safeties before cradling them.

Lee rolled a cigarette and lit it. Abe pulled a cigarette from the damp soft pack in the pocket of his t-shirt and used Lee's lighter to light it.

They watched Ike dutifully gather the guns. He heaped them around the Scout. Then he tried to open the crushed back door of the Scout. That didn't work. He stooped and began to the empty the remaining ammo from the guns, one by one. As each emptied, he tossed it through the glassless windows of the totaled Scout. Once he was finished, he came over to his dad and Lee and pulled the tobacco from his back pocket and rolled his own cigarette.

"Guns can go to scrap with the Scout," Ike said casually before lighting his cigarette.

The three now stood smoking and looking at the Dyson lot.

"Why'd you crush that old Scout?" Abe asked, kidding his friend. "Those are getting harder to come by. Always liked convertible trucks," Abe said and pointed with his cigarette at the Bronco. He noticed King inside the cab, frantic to be out, and began to march over to relieve the dog.

Lee hollered after him, "Had to get that Wild Bunch to drop arms and scatter if we was gonna get a bead on Shane to converse a moment or two."

Abe opened the cab door and let King out. The dog circled his master's knees once, ran toward the middle of the lawn near the crushed Scout, haunched, and began to shit.

"Was that part of Clifford's plan?" Abe had already figured correctly who would have put Lee up to it. "To smash the hell out of a car?"

"Nope," Wild Child said smiling proudly, "I seized that all on my own." He looked at Ike and winked.

Ike flipped Lee off and grinned and winked back. Abe walked back up alongside them.

MONDAY

Abe stood in the morning sun.

This summer was proving especially hot and it hadn't really rained since late April. The paper had shown last year how the old Woodville Cemetery tombstones emerged from the record low lake level. Woodville, Oklahoma had been purposefully flooded to build Lake Texoma. Abe wondered what the lake might let up this year if this year's drought continued.

Abe wasn't hurt by lack of rain. If anything the heat that come with it was good for his business—radiators and air conditioners going out and the like. Drought was never uncommon in these parts and Abe was grateful he'd never had to depend on rains to make his living in this country.

Abe's daddy's daddy had farmed and most of the family going back were farmers. After the Dust Bowl the Dyson kids of that generation abandoned the north Oklahoma family land to seek a livelihood elsewhere. Abe's daddy and uncle had made theirs doing what Abe now did—turning wrenches and fixing cars. They freed themselves of needing the rain to make a living.

Abe stared at his cracked lawn, waiting on the porch in the morning sun for Ike to come out, which he did within moments. They piled back in the Bronco and headed for the school.

The Dysons sat in the high school parking lot, mostly empty on account it was summer vacation. They stared at the building. If Ike'd kept going from where he'd started, this would have been his school, where he grew up. This is where his dad had gone. His mom too once her family moved back from California where she'd been born.

But that wasn't the road he stayed on and now he had wandered many paths. Too many to think on how one place like this could've changed things. Ike realized already how many places he'd been and seen over the years, felt intimate with even, were no longer in his recall.

Abe and Ike went inside the building. During summer the school was mostly empty and dark. Abe and Ike walked toward what appeared to be an open and lighted room down the main hallway. No security officer or office clerk was there to stop them.

As they approached each could see a piece of paper taped to the door frame on which was printed in permanent marker as neat as the author could manage: *Credit Recovery & G.E.D.*

Through the open door, Ike could see there was a mix of nine students. Seven appeared to be about high school aged—two Indian, four white, one Mexican. Two were older, maybe late thirties or early forties—one white, one black. All students were male and had their own desk and chair. Each appeared to be scribbling in or reading from a workbook in front of him, but each appeared to have a different workbook.

The scene was all too familiar to Ike, who'd taught in various schools over the years.

Once inside, Ike spotted another: what appeared to be an aging hippie sat behind a desk reading a book in a front corner of the room facing the students while they worked their workbooks.

Abe recognized Joe Dee Miller though it had been years since he'd run into him or seen him around town.

Ike noted Joe Dee Miller was reading a Larry McMurtry novel, but not one he'd heard of.

"Mornin', Joe Dee," Abe said, hoping Joe Dee would recognize him as well.

Joe Dee did recognize Abe Dyson and returned the greeting politely: "Hey, good mornin', Abe." Though he was kind, it was clear the eyes behind his little round glasses searched to reconcile the scene playing out before him. He noted the family resemblance in Ike, and wondered how long it'd been since he'd helped Abe sign his divorce at the court-house.

The students were quiet though certainly watched over their workbooks.

"What can I do for y'all?" Joe Dee asked noting Ike seemed as serious and ready to talk as Abe.

"Maybe we oughtta step in the hall," Ike suggested. Having worked in schools he knew how awkward personal conversations in front of students were.

"Sure," Joe Dee agreed.

Joe Dee pulled the class door to as he stepped into the hall behind Abe and Ike, but he did not let it shut all the way.

"I don't know what kinda pull I still got in such mat-ters," Joe Dee Miller offered with something of a heartbroken tone once Abe had explained as Clifford had told him to.

"Clifford Blow says you do," Abe protested. "Says it's not a problem of being in the good graces of the right people here, just going public with the right words and whatnot. You still go your words." The last part was not asked but asserted by Abe. Ike was struck with how vigilant his father had become in tone.

"And of course," Ike joined in not out of place, "You fought these folks before. You probably do know which newspaper writer would be friendly. Probably even know a decent politician who'd help such a cause. Anyway, if anyone could help us fight CW around these parts, it'd be you given you're the one has."

The Dyson men were determined.

"I do, and I do," Joe Dee said with a resigned nod at Abe and Ike, respectively.

"I'll drive," Ike said as they walked back toward the Bronco in the lot. Ike said it carefree and easy. The Dysons each felt great relief. Joe Dee Miller had agreed to save the day. At least, he would start the wheels in motion as Clifford had said he would.

Abe didn't realize until Ike made the offer that he'd been driving around the entire time he and his son had been riding around the past few days.

"Sure," Abe said, fine with it and not sure why he hadn't made the offer at some point already. Abe dug his ring out of his pocket and handed it to Ike.

The Bronco's square Ford-style ignition key was easy enough for Ike to find as soon as the keys were given. Ike walked to the driver's side door and opened it and crawled up in the Bronco.

Abe walked to the passenger side and opened its door and crawled in next to his son.

"You ever take the top off this thing?" Ike asked as he started the Bronco. He liked the pulse of the Ford V8 and glasspacks under him when he did so.

"Ever once in a while," Abe answered, though this was not true. He'd not pulled the top back off since the first few days after he'd finished rebuilding the Bronco.

"You did a nice job with this one. Really like the seats," Ike said, meaning the job Abe had done on his Bronco.

Abe had gotten the Bronco for eight hundred dollars because it had no rear end and its interior had housed a rat for some years and had been turned to shit. He had a spare rear-end in his scrap of parts that fit it and had it running down the road again in no time. He tuned its healthy Ford powerplant and cut out the rusty old muffler and threw on a dual exhaust with two thirteen inch glasspacks. On the inside he gutted the old rat chewed interior. Instead of finding a replacement for the back seat, he simply pulled out the seat brackets, pulled up the ratty carpet, sanded the entire back section, and sprayed it with black rubberized undercoating spray. It was a nice place for King to ride. Up front, Abe again ripped up carpet and sprayed the rubberized coating on the floor for a clean look. He replaced the pulverized old Bronco seats with a couple of sturdy tan buckets from an old Volvo wagon that pretty well matched the tan of the old dashboard which remained, though Abe had removed the instrument panel behind the steering wheel, replacing it with a piece of sheet metal for which he cut holes and inserted simple round gauges: a speedometer, a gas gauge, a temperature gauge. The entire inside was black and tan, and fairly well coordinated for a cheap rebuild. The outside remained brown, its sturdy factory paint still standing up to the Oklahoma sun save a fade spot or two.

As in high school, Abe had made a habit in his adulthood of buying rough used cars, fixing them up, driving them for a bit, then selling them for whatever profit he could get out of it after parts and all. He rarely drove a vehicle more than six months or so once he'd finished building it before he traded or sold it off. Every so often throughout the years he'd even traded for or bought back a couple of rebuilds long since sold off, then turned around a traded or sold them again.

But the Bronco was sticking around. Abe had finished it and begun driving it around town and on errands that didn't involve the tow truck as he'd always done. But no one ever made an offer to trade for or buy the Bronco and Abe never got the notion to let anyone know it might be for sale or trade.

It drove good as far as Ike could tell.

"Sara back tomorrow?" Ike asked Abe to make conversation.

"That's the plan far as I know," Abe replied with less reserve in his voice than he'd had since Ike'd been home. "She and her sister decided to stay out there an extra day to visit an old cousin used to live with 'em when they were younger."

"Nice," Ike said. Ike thought about his family as he drove. His dad. His grandfather. There was a line of something there, whatever he made of it.

He thought too about his mother. Everything had been so intense with her and now nothing for so long. Now that he was back, she was a phone call away. His stepfather of so long deserved to be found and visited as well. His stepmom would be home and he was looking forward to that. Ike looked at his dad.

There would be time. Time for this and time for that. Time.

He fixed his eyes on the road again.

Abe turned from the passenger window view and looked at his son. Ike drove with his right hand at the top of the wheel while his left arm rested on the open driver's window. Abe could see the hair on Ike's left arm blowing in the hot Oklahoma wind.

Ike turned onto 70. They were on the highway headed home now.

ACKNOWLEDGMENTS:

Previous excerpts have appeared in short story and vignette form in *Steel Toe Review*, *Crack the Spine*, and *Cheap Pop!* Many thanks to those editors and readers for their support. Special thanks to M. David Hornbuckle, Robert James Russell, and Jared Yates Sexton for their early reading and support. Finally, much appreciation to Amy Susan Wilson at Red Dirt Press for getting on board with the novel and her fantastic support as editor.